SECRETS IN

THE DARK

Ernest Morris

GOOD 2 GO PUBLISHING

SECRETS IN THE DARK
Written by Ernest Morris
Cover Design: Davida Baldwin, Odd Ball Designs
Typesetter: Mychea
ISBN: 978-1-947340-67-1
Copyright © 2021 Good2Go Publishing
Published 2021 by Good2Go Publishing
7311 W. Glass Lane • Laveen, AZ 85339
www.good2gopublishing.com
https://twitter.com/good2gobooks
G2G@good2gopublishing.com
www.facebook.com/good2gopublishing
www.instagram.com/good2gopublishing

Acknowledgments

First and foremost let me begin by sending out my condolences to everyone that lost a loved one because of this COVID-19 epidemic. We will rise up and conquer this because we're stronger.

Secondly, I would like to thank the man above for helping me understand how valuable talent is and that it shouldn't be wasted. It took me a while, but I now understand my worth. Every day I try to make a difference in this world, and as hard as it is to make a breakthrough, I finally feel like it's about to pay off. If I can show one person how important life is, then I have done my job.

I would like to thank everyone at GOOD2GO PUBLISHING for continuing to see the best in me. Even when I was at a low point in my life, you continued to trust me. It's because of you that I can walk around with my head held high and be proud of my success.

My goal is to be constructive, and not destructive.

There are many obstacles that we will face in our time on earth, but never back down, and most importantly, never give up. The only thing worse than being blind is having sight with no vision.

I would like to congratulate our new president, Mr. JOE BIDEN, and our first African American female vice president, Ms. Kamala Harris. Ms. Harris, you have broken barriers and inspired young women of all ages and races to believe in themselves, and know that anything is possible if you put your mind to it. Thank you!

Finally, I want to thank you, the readers. Without you, us authors wouldn't have a career. You made it possible for us to continue expressing our visions through writing. Please continue to support our brand and purchase my new novel: Breaking the Chains, on Amazon.com.

Prologue

Like the luxury co-ops and five-star French eateries located in Manhattan's Silk Stocking District, Benchley East Side Parking was outrageously exclusive. Tucked side by side and bumper to bumper within its four temperature-controlled underground levels beneath East Seventy-Seventh Street were several vintage Porsches, a handful of Lamborghinis, and even a pair of his-and-hers Bentleys.

The midnight-blue SL550 Mercedes convertible that squealed out of its car elevator at three minutes past noon that Saturday seemed tailor-fit to the high-rent neighborhood. So did the lean forty-something waiting by the garage's office when the sleek Mercedes stopped on a dime out front.

With his salt-and-pepper buzz cut, pressed khakis, silk navy golf shirt, and deep golden tan that suggested even deeper pockets, it was hard to tell if the car or its driver was being described by the purring Mercedes vanity plate.

"With all this heat, I figured you'd want the top down as usual, Mr. Covington," the smiling half-Hispanic, half-Asian garage attendant said as he bounced out and held open the wood-inlaid door. "Have a good one, now."

"Thanks, Tommy," Covington said, deftly slipping the man a ten as he slid behind the luxury sports car's iconic three-pronged steering wheel. "I'll give it a shot."

The fine leather seat slammed luxuriously into Covington's back as he launched the convertible with a high torque snarl down East Seventy-Seventh Street and out onto Fifth Avenue. The crisp, almost sweet smell of Central Park's pine oaks and dogwoods fused harmoniously with the scent of the hand-stitched leather. At Fifty-Ninth Street, the park's treetops gave way to the ornate fairy-tale facade of the Plaza Hotel.

"Let me find something to listen to," he said, channel searching on his XM Radio. Once he found what he was looking for, he turned up the volume.

"That'll work."

Moments later, along both sides of the upscale boulevard, glittering signs began to flick past like a Vanity Fair magazine come to life: Tiffany's, Chanel, Zegna, Pucci, Fendi, Louis Vuitton. Outside the stores, swarms of summer Saturday tourists took pictures and stood gaping as if they were having trouble believing they were standing in the very center of the capital of the world.

But the world's most expensive avenue might as well have been a dirt road through a shitkicker's cornfield as far as Covington was concerned. Behind the mirrored lenses of his glasses, he kept his gray eyes locked level and forward, his mind blank. It was his one true talent. In his life, every victory had come down to singleness of purpose, his ability to focus, to leave out everything but the matter at hand.

Even so, he felt his pulse skitter when he finally arrived at his destination, the New York Public Library's main branch on the west side of Fifth Avenue between Forty-First and Forty-Second

Streets. In fact, as he slowed, he felt his adrenaline surge, and his heart began to beat almost painfully in time with the car's indicator.

Even Olivier had stage fright, he reminded himself as he carefully turned onto East Forty-Third Street. Sean Combs. Jay Z. All men felt fear. The distinction of great and worthy men like him was the ability to manage it, to act despite the fact that it was breathing down their necks.

By the time he tucked the Mercedes into a parking spot in front of an ice cream truck half a block farther east, he felt somewhat better. To ground himself completely, he patiently watched the hardtop glide into place over his head, precise, symmetrical, a glorious harmony of moving parts. By the time it locked itself down, his fear was still there, but he knew he could man it.

Move it, Mr. Covington, he thought. He lifted the heavy laptop bag from the passenger seat footwell and opened the door.

"It's now or never," he mumbled, shutting the

door.

Passing under the grand Beaux-Arts arched portico and through a pair of revolving doors of the library, Covington immediately noticed that the steely-eyed ex-cop who usually worked the front hall on Saturdays wasn't there. Instead, there was a young summer hire slouch in a tight blazer. Even better. The bored-looking bridge and tunneler waved Covington through before he could even lift a finger to his bag's zipper.

The hushed Rose Reading Room on the 3rd floor was about the size of a professional football field. It was rimmed with ten-foot high caramel-colored wooden shelves and lit by brass Rococo chandeliers that hung down from its fifty-one-foot-high, mural-painted, coffered ceiling. Covington stepped past table after long table of very serious-looking thirtysomethings and fortysomethings, earbuds snug in their ears as they stared intently at laptop screens. Graduate students and ardent self-improvers. No Hamptons this summer weekend for this studious bunch.

He found a seat at the last table along the north wall, with his back to the door of the Rare Book Division of the Brooke Russell Astor Reading Room. He pretended to play sudoku on his iPhone until the only other person at the study table, a pregnant Asian woman in a sweat suit, got up twenty minutes later.

As she waddled away, Mr. Covington took one last deep breath and slowly released it. Then he slipped on a pair of rubber surgical gloves under the table and slid the bomb out of the laptop bag. It looked exactly like an Apple Notebook seventeen-inch laptop except that there was a hollowed-out space where the keyboard, mouse pad, and computer guts had once been. In their place now sat two kilograms of T4, the Italian version of the plastic explosive RDX. On top of the pale vanilla-colored plastic explosive sat another two-inch-thick layer of barbed stainless steel roofing nails, like a double helping of silver sprinkles on the devil's ice cream cone.

There was a gel-like adhesive already attached to the device's bottom. He pressed the bomb firmly down in front of him, gluing it securely to the library desk. The detonator cap had already been inserted into the explosive and now merely awaited the final connection to an electrical charge, which would occur when someone discovered the laptop and made the mistake of opening the cover.

Tied just inside the cover with a snug lanyard knot made of fishing line was a mercury switch, an ingenious little thermometer-like glass tube that was used in vending machine alarms. When the lid was closed, you could play Frisbee with the IED. Once the lid rose two inches, however, the liquid mercury would spill to the switch's bottom, cover its electrical leads, and initiate instant detonation.

Mr. Covington imagined the bomb's massive shockwave ripping through the crowded Rose Reading Room, blowing apart everything and everyone within forty feet and sending a killing wall of shrapnel in every direction at four times the speed of sound. He peeled off his gloves and stood with the now empty laptop bag, careful not to touch anything. He crossed the room and stepped quickly out of the exit without looking back.

"It has begun," he thought with a feeling of magnificent relief as he found the marble stairs. From here on in, it would be all about timing. A race against the clock, so to speak.

"On your mark. Get set. Blow," Mr. Covington whispered happily to himself, and began to take the stairs down two at a time.

CHAPTER
1

"I GOT ENEMIES, GOT A LOT OF ENEMIES," I rapped along with Drake, really getting into it waving my hands. "Got a lot of people trying to take me off this energy."

It seemed to me like an appropriate song for the way I was feeling today. Unfortunately, I was the only one that thought so. A split second later, a fusillade of groans and boos sailed back from my daughters. They didn't like when I rapped. They thought I was too old to be doing that. I told them that forty was the new thirty. They laughed and sucked their teeth at me. Still I bowed and continued, displaying my trademark smile under pressure. Never let them see you sweat, even on summer vacation, which is really hard when you think about it.

My name is E. J. Morris, and I'm now an NYPD detective. I transferred out here from Pennsylvania because I wanted my two daughters to get the New York experience. Who am I kidding? I moved out here because I was a Giants and Knicks fan. Plus, they offered me a big raise to take the helm of their special task force, and I gladly accepted it. I needed something different anyway.

Besides me and my daughters, I had my new girlfriend and her two kids with us. She also wanted a change of scenery. It was week two of my much-needed family vacation out in Breezy Point, Queens, and I was definitely in full goof-off mode. It was more crowded than a rabbit's warren, but it was also nonstop swimming and hot dogs and board games, and beer and bonfires at night.

No emails, no electronics. No modern imple-ments of any kind except for the temperamental A/C and a saltwater-rusted bicycle. I watched as Shayana, the baby of the two, chased a tern, or maybe it was a piping plover, on the shoulder of the road. Time was flying, but I was making the most of it. As usual. For a single father, making the most of things pretty much went without saying.

"If you guys don't like Drake, how about a little Meek Mills?" I said to my family. "Look, I be riding through my old hood—"

"No, Dad, stop singing please," Le'Shea said. "You're embarrassing us."

"Come on, sing with me," I said playfully, grabbing her hands. She wasn't going for none of that though. My baby pulled away from me and ran.

We were actually heading to Oceanside Avenue for five o'clock mass. Did I mention that my girlfriend turned me from Christian to Catholic. I loved her that much that I wanted her to see that I could sacrifice some of my own beliefs, to adjust to hers. Besides, vacation was no excuse for missing mass, especially for us. My girlfriend's grandfather, in addition to being a comedian, was a late-to-the-cloth priest.

"Would ya look at that," Seamus said, standing on the sandy steps of St. Edmund's and tapping his watch when we finally arrived. "It must be six of the apostles. Of course not. They'd be on time for mass. Get in here, heathens, before I forget that I'm not a man of violence."

"Sorry, Father," Amy said, a sentiment that was repeated five more times in rough ascending order by Jake, Anima, Le'Shea, Shayana, and of course yours truly. Seamus put his hand on my elbow as I was fruitlessly searching for a pew that would seat a family of six.

"Just to let you know, I'm offering mass for Ashley today," he said.

Ashley was my late wife, the woman who gave me two wonderful daughters before falling to some throat disease that took her from me too soon. I used to wake up some mornings, reaching out for a moment before my brutal shitty aha moment that I was alone. That was before Amy moved in. It was touching that he would do something like this and didn't even know anything about her. He only knew the things that me and Amy had told him. I smiled and nodded as I patted Seamus's wrinkled cheek.

"I wouldn't have it any other way, Monsignor," I said as the organ started.

The service was quick but quite nice—especially the part where we prayed for Ashley. I'm not in line to become pope anytime soon, but I like mass. It's calming, restorative. A moment to review where you've gone wrong over the past week and maybe think about getting things back on track. Call it psychotherapy. Therapy for this Afro American psycho, anyway.

All in all, I came back out into the sun feeling pretty calm and upbeat. Which lasted about as long as it took the holy water I blessed myself with to dry.

"Get him! Hit him harder! Yeah, boyyyyzzzz!" some kid was yelling.

There was some commotion alongside the church. Through the departing crowd and cars, I saw about half a dozen kids squaring off in the parking lot.

"Look out, Jake!" someone yelled.

"Jake?" I thought. Wait a second. That was one

of my kids! I rushed into the brawl, with my soon-to-be daughter Anima on my heels. There was a pile of kids swinging and kicking on the sun-bleached asphalt. I started grabbing shirt collars, yanking kids away, putting my NYPD riot police training to good use. I found Jake at the bottom of the scum, red-faced and near tears.

"You want some more, bitch? Come and get it!" one of the kids who'd been kicking Jake yelled as he lurched forward. Jake, our resident bookworm, was fourteen. The tall, pudgy kid with the Mets cap askew looked at least seventeen.

"Back it up!" I yelled at the punk with a lot of cop in my voice and more in my eyes. Jake, tears gone, just angry now, thumbed some blood from his nostril. "What happened?"

"That jerk called Anima something bad."

"What?"

"A whore."

I turned and glared at the big kid with the even bigger mouth. I really felt like knocking the fat kid's hat back straight with a slap. Instead, I quickly thought of another idea.

"In that case," I said, staring at the delinquent. "Kick his ass."

"My pleasure," Jake said, trying to lunge from my grip.

At the very last second, I pulled him back so he couldn't attack. Violence never solved anything. At least when there were witnesses around. Twenty or thirty loyal St. Edmund's parishioners had stopped to watch the proceedings.

"What's your name?" I said as I walked over and personally got in the kid's face.

"Flaherty," the kid said with a stupid little smile.

"That's Gaelic for dumb-ass," Anima said by my shoulder.

"What's your problem, Flaherty?" I said.

"Who has a problem?" Flaherty said. "Maybe it's you guys. Maybe the Point isn't your cup of tea. Maybe you should bring your rainbow coalition family out to the Hamptons. You know, Puff Daddy?

7

That crowd?"

I took a deep breath and released it even more slowly. This kid was getting on my nerves. Even though he was just a teen, my somewhat cleansed soul was wrestling valiantly not to commit the sin of wrath.

"I'm going to tell you this one time, Flaherty. Stay away from my kids, or I'm going to give you a free ride in my police car."

"Wow, you're a cop. I'm scared," Flaherty said. "This is the point. I know more cops than you do, old man."

I stepped in closer to him, close enough to head butt, anyway.

"Do any of them work at Spofford?" I said in his ear.

Spofford was New York's infamous juvie hall. By his swallow, I thought I'd finally gotten through.

"Whatever," Flaherty said, walking away.

"Why me?" I thought, turning away from the stunned crowd of churchgoers. You never saw this kind of crap on TLC. And what the hell did he mean by old man?

"Jake?" I said as I started leading my kids back along the hot, sandy road toward the promised land of our saltbox.

"Yes?"

"Stay away from that kid."

"Anima?" I said a few seconds later.

"Yes," she said with the softest voice.

"Keep an eye on that kid."

CHAPTER 2

ABOUT AN HOUR LATER, I WAS OUT ON THE back deck on my ancestral home, working the ancestral grill full-tilt boogie. Dogs on the warming rack. Cheese slices waiting to be applied to the rows of sizzling freshly ground burgers. Blue smoke in my face, ice-cold bottle of water in my hand. We were so close to the water, I could actually hear the rhythmic roll and crash of saltwater dropping onto hard-packed sand.

If I leaned back on the creaky rail of the deck and turned to my left, I was actually able to see the Atlantic two blocks to the east. If I turned to the right, to the other side of Jamaica Bay, I could see the sun starting its long descent toward the skyline of Manhattan, where I worked. I hadn't had to look in that direction for over a week now and was praying that it stayed that way until the first of August.

No doubt about it. My world was a fine place and worth fighting for. Maybe not in church parking lots, but still. I heard something on XM Radio behind me. It was that song by Jeremih, "Love Don't Change." I laughed as I remembered dancing to it with Ashley at our wedding. I cranked it. You better believe I was preoccupied with music. No internet, so this was it.

"Bets to you, Padre," I heard Trent say behind me.

Inside at the kitchen table, a tense game of Texas hold 'em was underway. A lot of candy had been trading hands all evening.

"All right, hit me," Seamus said.

"Grandpa, this isn't blackjack," Anima complained with a giggle.

"Go fish?" Seamus tried.

I thought about what my new young friend Flaherty had said about my multicultural family. It was me and my two daughters who were black, and Amy and her two kids who were white. What was wrong with that, I don't know. It was funny how wrong people got it. I turned as Le'Shea opened the sliders to the deck. I wanted to joke until I noticed her look.

She was holding my work cell phone in her hand, and it was vibrating. I threw a panicked glance back toward the Manhattan skyline. I knew it. Things had been too good for too long, not to mention way too quiet.

"Answer it," I finally said to her, pissed.

"Morris," she said, trying to disguise her voice. "Gimme a crime scene."

"You crazy," I said, snatching the phone out of her hand. "That was my daughter, and you can keep the crime scene."

"I wish I could," my new boss, inspector Miriam Schwartz, said.

I closed my eyes. "Idiot! I knew we should have gone to Florida."

"I'm on vacation," I protested.

"We both are, but this is big, E. J. Homeland Security big. Just got off the phone with Manhattan Borough Command. Someone left one hell of a bomb at the main branch of the New York Public Library."

I almost dropped the phone as a pulse of cold crackled down my spine and the backs of my legs. My stomach churned as memories of what happened at the World Trade Center during 9/11 began to flash before my eyes. Fear, sorrow, useless anger, the end-of-the-world stench of scorched metal all over the place. "This can't be happening again," I thought.

"A bomb?" I said slowly. "Is it armed?"

"No, thank God. It's disarmed. But it's 'sophisticated as shit,' to quote Paul Jones from Bomb Squad. There was a note with it."

"I hate fucking notes. Was it a sorry one?" I said.

"No such luck, E. J." Miriam said. "It said, 'This wasn't supposed to go boom, but the next one will.' Something like that. The commissioner wants Major Case on this. I need my major player. That's why you were transferred here, E. J. They're waiting on you."

"Yeah, who isn't?" I said, dropping the spatula as my burgers burned.

• • •

As I rolled under the bridge back into the city toward my date with a bomb on Forty-Second Street, for some strange reason, I couldn't stop thinking of what could have happened if that bomb went off. I skipped the backup FDR Drive and took the side streets, St. James to the Bowery to Park Avenue South. Half a block west of Grand Central Terminal, wooden NYPD sawhorses had been set up, cordoning off Forty-Second Street in both directions. Behind the yellow tape, a crowd of summering Asian and European tourists stood front row center, cameras aloft, taking in some action.

After I badged my way through the outer perimeter, I parked behind a Seventeenth Precinct radio car half a block south of Forty-Second Street. As I was getting out, I spotted a shiny new blue Crown Vic and a couple of tall and neat-looking guys in JTTF polo shirts sitting on its hood, talking on their cellphones.

I doubted they were here to play polo. Calling in the Joint Terrorism Task Force Feds at the slightest hint of the T-word was standard operating procedure in our jittery post-9/11 metropolis. The Feds didn't seem too impressed with me or my gold shield as I walked past them. I knew I should have put a jacket on over my thin shirt. When I arrived at the corner diagonal to the library, I could see more barricades far down Forty-Second Street at Sixth Avenue and three blocks in both directions up and down Fifth Avenue. The silence and lack of traffic on what was usually one of the busiest intersections on earth was zombie movie eerie.

"¿Sarge, qué pasa?" I said, showing my badge to the Hispanic female uniform at the inner perimeter's aluminum gate.

"Seems like some nut forgot his overdue books, so he returned a booby-trapped bomb to the library instead," she said as I signed into her crime scene logbook she was carrying.

"Anyone get hurt?"

"No, but we got the place evacked, including Bryant Park. The bomb nuts are inside. Midtown North Squad took a bus of witnesses and staff back to the precinct, but I heard it ain't looking too good."

Among the library's columns and fountains, I passed nervous-looking Midtown North Task Force and Seventeenth Precinct uniforms. Some of the cops were holding what appeared to be radar guns but were really radiation detectors. An unmarked van geared with God knows what kind of testing equipment was parked at the curb.

At the front entrance of the library, a redheaded guy in a white marshmallow man Tyvek suit walked out with a yellow Lab on a leash. The Labrador wasn't a seeing-eye dog, I knew, but an EDC, an explosive detection canine. I loved dogs, just not at crime scenes. A dog at a crime scene means bombs or dead bodies, and I wasn't particularly jazzed about seeing either one. "Ain't looking too good" seemed like the mid-summer evening's theme, I thought as I climbed the stairs between the two giant stone lions.

CHAPTER 3

A BIG BALD GUY WITH A TWIRLY BLACK mustache and tactical blue fatigues met me beneath the landmark building's massive portico. With his mustache, Paul Jones bore a striking resemblance to the guy on the Bomb Squad's logo patch, depicting a devil-may-care Red Baron-looking guy riding a bomb in front of the skyline of Manhattan.

"We got the parked cars and street furniture sniffed, so I'm pretty sure there aren't any secondary devices," Jones said. "Think about it. Draw in the first responders with a decoy. That's what I'd do. Look at all these windows. Some jihadist could be behind any one of them right now with his finger on the button, watching us, aching for that glorious thump and flash of holy light."

"Christ, Paul, please," I said, clutching my chest. "I skipped my Lipitor this morning."

Jones and his guys were the world's elite in bomb handling, as tight and quick and efficient as an NGO team. More so probably since the penalty box on this squad was made of pine. All cops are crazy, but these guys took the cake.

"Fine, fine. You ready to see the main attracttion?" Jones said, ushering me through the library door with a gracious wave of his hand.

"No, but let's do it anyway," I said, taking a breath.

We passed another half dozen even more nervous-looking cops as we crossed the library's monster marble entry hall to a flight of stone stairs. More bomb techs were helping their buddy out of the green astronaut-like Kevlar bomb suit in the ostentatious wood-paneled rotunda on the 3rd floor. Another guy was putting away the four-wheeler wireless robot and the X-ray equipment.

"Uh, won't we need that stuff?" I asked. Jones shook his head.

"We already deactivated the device. Actually, we

didn't have to. It wasn't meant to go off. Here, I'll show you what I'm talking about."

I reluctantly followed him into the cavernous reading room. The space resembled a ballroom and was even more impressive than the entry hall, with its massive arched windows, chandeliers, and nineteenth-century indoor football field of books. The last library table in the northern end zone of the elaborate room was covered by a thick orange Kevlar bomb-suppression blanket. I felt my pulse triple and my hands clench involuntarily as Jones lifted it off.

In the center of the table was what looked like a silver laptop. Then I saw the nails and wires and claylike plastique explosive where the keyboard should have been, and shivered. On the screen, the chilling and redundant words I AM A BOMB flashed on and off before the scrolling message:

THIS WASN'T SUPPOSED TO GO BOOM,

BUT THE NEXT ONE WILL. I SWEAR IT

ON POOR LAWRENCE'S EYES.

"This guy has some style," Jones said, looking

almost admiringly at the bomb. "It's basically like a Claymore mine. Two K's of plastique behind all these nails, one huge mother of a shotgun shell. All wired to a nifty motion-sensitive mercury switch, only the second one I've ever seen. He even glued it to the desk so someone would have to open it and spill the mercury."

"How . . . interactive of him," I said, shaking my head.

By far, my least favorite part of the message was the ominous reference to the next one. I was afraid of that. It looked like somebody wanted to play a little game with the NYPD. Considering I was on vacation, unless it was beach ball, I really wasn't that interested in games.

"He used a real light touch with a soldering gun to wire it up to the battery. He must know computers as well, because even though the hard drive is missing, he was able to program his little greeting card through the computer's firmware internal operating system."

"Why didn't it go off?" I said.

"He cut one of the wires and capped both ends in order for it not to go off, thank God."

"Wow!"

"Security guy said the room was packed, like it is every Saturday. This would have killed a dozen people easily, E. J. Maybe two dozen. The blast wave itself from this much plastique could collapse a house."

We stared silently at the scrolling message.

"It almost sounds like a poem, doesn't it?" Jones said.

"Yeah," I said, taking out my iPhone and speed-dialing my boss. "I've even seen the style before. It's called psychotic pentameter."

"Tell me what we got, E. J.," Miriam said a moment later.

"Miriam," I said, staring at the flashing I AM A BOMB, "what we got here is a problem."

• • •

The Alexander Hotel just off Madison on Forty-Fourth was understaffed, overpriced, and excessively seedy. All the grim, peeling walls, off-white towels, and pot smoke and piss stench $175 a night could buy. Sitting cross-legged on the desk that he'd moved in front of his top-floor room's window, Covington slowly panned his camera across the columns and entablatures of the landmark marble library seventeen stories below.

The $11,000 Nikkor super-zoom lens attached to his 35-millimeter digital camera could make faces distinguishable at up to a mile. At a block and a half, with the incredibly vivid magnification, Covington could see the sweat droplets on the first responders' nervous faces.

Beside him on the desk was a laptop, a digital stopwatch, and a legal tablet filled with the neat shorthand notes he'd been taking for the past several hours. Evacuation procedures. Response times. He'd left the window open so that he could hear the sirens, immerse himself in the confusion on the street. He was meticulously photographing the equipment inside the open back door of the Bomb Squad van when someone knocked on the door. Freaking, Covington swung immediately off the desk. He lifted something off the bed as he passed.

It was a futuristic-looking Austrian Steyr AUG submachine gun, all thirty 5.56 NATO rounds already cocked, locked, and ready to rock.

"Yes?" Covington said as he lifted the assault rifle to his shoulder.

"Room service. The coffee you ordered, sir," said a voice behind the door.

No way anyone could be on to him this quickly! Had someone in another window seen him? What the hell was this? He leveled the machine gun's long suppressed barrel center mass on the door.

"I didn't order anything," Covington said.

"No?" the voice said. There was a pause. A long one. In his mind, Covington saw a SWAT cop in a ski mask applying a breaching charge on the door. Covington eyed down the barrel, muscles bunching on his wiry forearms, finger hovering over the trigger, heart stopped, waiting.

"Oh, shit—er, I mean, sugar," the hotel worker said finally. "My mistake. It's an eleven, not a seventeen. So sorry, sir. I can't read my own handwriting. Sorry to have bothered you."

"More than you'll ever know," Covington thought, rubbing the tension out of the bridge of his nose. He waited until he heard the double roll of the elevator door down the outside hall before he lowered the gunstock off his shoulder.

A man was standing talking to the Bomb Squad chief down on the library's pavilion when Covington arrived back to the zoom lens. After clicking a close-up shot with the camera, he smiled as he examined the looming face on the screen. It was him. Finally. Detective E. J. Morris. New York's newest member, and quote, unquote New York's finest, had arrived at last.

The feeling of satisfaction that hummed through Covington was almost the same as the psychic glee he got when he'd perfectly anticipated a counter-move in a game of chess. Covington grinned as he squinted through the viewfinder, watching Morris. He knew all about him, his high-profile Philadelphia and Scranton career, his very well-respected family.

Covington shot a glance over at the rifle sitting on the bed. From this distance, he could easily put a tight grouping into the cop with the suppressed rifle. Blow him to pieces, splatter them all over the marble columns and steps. "Wouldn't that stir the pot?" Covington thought, taking his eyes off the gun. All in due time. Stick to the plan, and stay with the mission.

"Stay tuned, my friends," Covington said, allowing himself a brief smile as he clicked another shot of the clueless cops. "There's much more where this came from. In Lawrence's honor."

CHAPTER
4

I DIDN'T HAVE A CARE IN THE WORLD AS I fought the Saturday-night gridlock on the BQE back to Breezy Point. No, wait a second. That's what I was wishing were true. My real mood was closer to depressed and deeply disturbed after my face time with the sophisticated booby-trapped bomb and cryptic e-note.

Jones and his crew had ended up cutting off the entire library tabletop to transport the bomb out to their range in the Bronx. A quick call to Midtown North revealed that no one in the library or its staff had noticed anyone or anything particularly out of the ordinary. With the absence of security cameras at the location, we were left with basically nada, except for one extremely sophisticated improvised explosive device and a seemingly violent nut's promise to deliver more.

To add insult to injury, a briefing about the incident had been called for the morning down at One Police Plaza, my presence required. "I hate seemingly violent nuts," I thought as I got on the Belt Parkway. "Especially ones who really seem to know what they're doing." Even though it was ten and way past everyone's bedtime, all the windows of the beach house were lit as I parked the SUV and came up our sandy path. I could hear my kids inside laughing as Seamus held court. It sounded like a game of Pictionary, the old codger's favorite. He was a born ham.

I went around back and grabbed a couple of beers to wind down on the porch. When I came back, I spotted a good-looking redhead sitting on the steps. "Hey, wait a second," I thought after my double-take. "That's not just a good-looking redhead; that's my beautiful woman Amy Ciborosky."

"Psst," I called to her, waving temptingly from the shadows. "Come on before someone sees us."

We crossed the two blocks to the beach and

walked out on the dunes, drinking, taking our time, and enjoying the moonlit sky.

"Where we going?"

"Just come on," I told her.

We made a left and headed north toward a firemen's bar nearby called the Sugar Bowl that we'd been to a couple of nights after the kids had gone to sleep. I just really needed some time alone with this beautiful woman, and this was the perfect opportunity.

"How's the thesis coming?" I said as we walked along the beach.

Amy was taking classes to become an RN. She liked helping people and figured if she got her degree, she could work at one of the hospitals. They could sure use the help. She was in the midst of getting her master's from Columbia. Which made her as smart and sophisticated as she was pretty and kind. She was truly a special person. Why, her and her kids insisted on hanging around me and my kids, giving us a chance to be in their lives. I was planning on making it permanent real soon hopefully.

"This is nice," she said.

"Well I'm glad you like it," I said. As we approached the loud, crowded bar, Amy stopped.

"Let's keep going, E. J. It's so nice out," she said, hooking a right and walking across some more dunes and seagrass down toward the Atlantic. I liked the sound of that. No dead air this time.

"If you insist," I told her.

We were strolling beside the rumbling waves at the shoreline when she dropped her drink. We went to grab it at the same time and bumped heads as the surf splattered around our ankles.

"Are you okay?" I said, holding her by her shoulders.

We were so close, our chins were almost touching. We both looked into each other's eyes and started kissing. Softly, sweetly. I put my arms around her waist and pulled her toward me. She was lighter than usual, softer, so delicate. After a minute as we continued to slowly kiss, I felt her warm hand making its way inside my pants. She grabbed my hard-on and gently massaged it.

"Wait," I whispered in her ear. "Let's get comfortable."

I took off my shirt and laid it over the sand so she could lie down. She removed her pants, giving me a wonderful view of her vagina. After all this time, Amy still had the most beautiful lips I ever saw, and they were poking out through the leopard thong she wore. She lie down on the shirt, spreading her legs so I could dive right in. The thrill of knowing that someone could walk past and see what we were doing only intensified the excitement.

I pulled her thong to the side and planted my tongue on her clit, flicking it just how she liked it. Then I blew into her hole. It drove her crazy. She began convulsing, grabbing my head, trying to push my face deeper into her love box. I licked, sucked, and licked some more, like I was feasting on a home-cooked meal. Amy felt herself about to cum, and tried to push away, but I held firmly to her waist. I wanted to suck her juices out of her body.

"I'm cuummmming," she yelled out. "Oh my God."

It squirted all in my mouth. I wasn't done with her yet though. I wanted her to cum at least three more times before I got mine. A couple was walking on the beach, about fifty yards from us holding hands. When they saw us making out, instead of them running away, they started doing the same right there.

"I think we have an audience," I whispered.

Amy was so turned on from my tongue that she didn't care what I was talking about or who was there. The only thing that mattered was getting that next orgasm. She pushed my head back down between her legs, to her drenched pussy. Even after she had her orgasm, it still smelled so good. I moved up and sucked on her breasts one at a time. Her nipples were hard as rocks.

When I looked over at the couple watching us, they were already partaking in some foreplay of their own. I tried not to pay them any attention, but it was hard considering that they were now completely naked.

"They are really into it," I said, giving a head nod for Amy to look in that direction.

"I'm not worried about them. You need to be handling your business right here," she replied, pulling her pussy lips apart.

That was all I needed to see. I was inside her in a matter of seconds. She moaned and screamed so loud that if that couple didn't hear us before, they sure heard us now. It didn't take long before we were both cumming all over each other. We got dressed and headed back home without a care in the world.

CHAPTER 5

IT SEEMED LIKE I'D JUST FALLEN ASLEEP WHEN my eyes shot open in the dark, my heart racing. Confused, I lifted my cell phone off the bedside table to see if its ringing was what woke me up. That's when I heard glass breaking.

"Dad!" Shayana called from down the hall.

"Shhhh, stay in here with Amy," I told her.

It was coming from the dorm. I jumped out of bed and began turning on lights as I ran. Beside Jake's bed by the bay window, there was broken glass and a chunk of concrete. I ran to the window, then ducked as a beer bottle ricocheted off the glassless frame and whizzed past my ear. I could see a small car parked in front of the house with its lights off. Two or three people were in it.

"You suck, Morris!" called a voice. "Get out of the Point while you still can!"

On the wings of hate, I flew out of the room toward the front door. I was past pissed, more like enraged. Those bastards could have hurt or killed one of my kids. In bare feet, wearing just my boxer shorts, I ran out the front door, picking up an aluminum baseball bat from the porch as I ran.

The car's engine raced as I hit the street. Its tires barked as the car peeled out. I could hear teenage kids inside laughing and yelling. Instead of trying to get the plate, like the trained law enforcement professional I was, I went another route. I hauled back and threw the bat as hard as I could at the car's taillights. It clinked across the empty asphalt as they rounded the corner.

I ran to the corner, but there was no sign of them. They'd gotten away. I was absolutely wide awake as I stood there in the dark. My adrenaline was definitely pumping. I didn't care how old Flaherty was. No one messed with my kids. I really felt like killing someone. It would be my secret in the dark, because no one would ever find out about it.

Le'Shea came up behind me as I was retrieving the bat I threw.

"Was that the Flaherty kid, Dad?" she asked. "Had to be, right?"

"I didn't see any faces, but it's a pretty safe assumption," I replied.

"I asked around about him, Dad. They say he's bad news. Actually, his whole family is crazy. He has five brothers, each one badder than the next. They even have a pit bull. Someone said they're Westies, Dad."

I thought about that. The Westies were what was left of the Irish mafia, latent thugs and gangsters who still ran some rackets on the West Side of Manhattan. One of their signature moves was dismembering bodies. And we'd apparently just gotten into a feud with them? Le'Shea looked at me, worried. I put an arm around her shoulders.

"Look at me, Le'Shea," I said, indicating my lack of attire. "Do I look the same to you? In the mean-time, try to stay away from them. I'ma tell your step-brother and sister the same. I'll take care of it."

I wasn't sure how, but I kept that to myself. Everyone, and I mean everyone, was awake and on the porch as we came back. Some joker from the cottage across the street gave a cat-calling whistle out the window at my shirtless body as I stepped up the stairs.

"Daddy, get in here!" Shayana commanded. "You can't walk around in just your underpants."

"You're right, princess," I said, actually managing a smile. "Daddy forgot."

● ● ●

I left for work early the next morning. Which, if you're vacationing in the ass end of Queens and want to avoid the traffic back into the city, means being in the car by a bleary-eyed five thirty. I hadn't gotten much sleep thanks to the late-night cinder block delivery from the Breezy Point welcoming committee. My family was pretty shaken up, and though I didn't want to admit it, so was I.

The kid Flaherty really did seem kind of crazy, and I, more than most, knew what crazy people were capable of. After the incident, I had called the local One Hundredth Precinct, or the "1-0-0" in cop parlance, who'd sent over a radio car about half an hour later. We'd filled out a report, but from the shift commander's ho-hum expression, I didn't get the impression that finding the culprits was too high on his night's priority list. So much for professional courtesy. The best we could do was have a guy come fix the window later that day and hope that was the end of it.

I checked my iPhone in the driveway before leaving and learned that the morning's case-meeting locale had been changed from NYPD's One Police Plaza headquarters to the fancy new NYPD Counter-terrorism Bureau on the Brooklyn/Queens border. Though I was glad I didn't have to drive as far, I didn't like how quickly the case was escalating. My dwindling hopes of salvaging the remainder of my vacation seemed to be diminishing at an increasingly rapid clip.

As I was coming in, Miriam suggested we meet for breakfast at a diner near the Counterterrorism HQ beforehand to get on the same page. I arrived first and scored us a window booth overlooking an expensive junkyard vista. A muted Channel Two news story about the bomb threat was playing on the TV behind the counter. An overhead shot of the cop-covered public library was followed by another one of a pretty female reporter standing by a police barricade.

A truck driver in the adjacent booth glared at me as I loudly groaned into my white porcelain cup. I knew this was coming. Media heat meant heat on the mayor, which I knew through bitter experience would roll quickly in one direction: downhill, straight at me.

About ten minutes later, I watched from the window as my boss, Miriam, got out of her Impala. Stylish and athletic and irritatingly serene, Miriam looked more like a hot upscale soccer mom than a razor-sharp city cop.

Despite the fact that she had ordered me back from my vacay, I still liked my feisty new boss. Coming into this unit, my status was right under hers. Running the Major Case Squad, the Delta Force of the NYPD, was a near-impossible job. Not only was Miriam's head constantly on the chopping block with high-profile cases, but she had the added challenge of having to garner the respect and loyalty of the department's most elite detectives, who were often prima donnas.

Somehow Miriam, a former air force pilot, managed to pull it off with wily intelligence, humor, and tact. She also backed her people unconditionally and took absolutely no one's shit. Including mine, unfortunately.

"What's the story, morning glory?" my boss said as she sat down.

"Let's see. Hmm. Today's headline, I guess, is 'Vacationing Cop Gets Screwed,'" I said.

"Hey, I feel you, dawg. I was up in Cape Cod,

sipping a fuzzy navel when they called me."

"Who's was it? Anyone I know?" I asked.

"A gentlewoman never tells," she said with a sly wink. "Anyway, hope your shoes are shined. Sander Flaum from Intel is going to be at this powwow, as well as the counterterrorism chief, Cardi, and a gaggle of nervous Feds. You're today's featured speaker, so don't let them trip you up."

"Wait a second. Back up," I said. "I'm the primary detective on the case? So now I'm on vacation when? Nights?"

"Ah, Mike," Miriam said as the waitress poured her a coffee. "You Irish have such a way with words. Yeats, Joyce, and now you."

"For a nice Jewish girl from Brooklyn, you're not too bad at throwing the blarney around when you have to," I said. "Seriously, two chiefs? Why all the heavies on a Sunday?"

"The lab came back on the explosive. It's T-four from Europe—from Italy apparently. You know how squirrelly the commissioner gets about anything terrorist related."

The new commissioner, Ken Rodin, was a pugnacious, old-school former beat cop who still wore a .38 in an ankle holster above his Italian wingtips. With crime down in the city, his primary directive, some said his obsession, was to prevent another terrorist act during his watch. Which wasn't as paranoid as it might sound, considering NYC was still a terrorist organization, Top of the Pops, so to speak.

"Though it's still far from conclusive that this is a terrorist thing, we have to go through the DEFCON 1 motions for the time being. There's been smoke coming out of my iPhone all night."

"Is McGirth going to be there?"

Tom McGinnis, or McGirth, as he was more casually known due to his not-so-girlish figure, was the department's chief of detectives, Miriam's boss, and perhaps the most egregious power-hungry ballbuster in the NYPD. Miriam rolled her eyes in affirmation.

"What's up with bullshit internal politics?" I said. "What happened to the commissioner's pep talk last month about how the mayor wanting a new role for the Major Case? Kick ass, no politics, just results? Ring the bell?"

"Yeah, well, the mayor and the commish aren't going to be at the meeting, unfortunately," Miriam said. "It's our sorry lot to deal with the department's evil henchmen. Why am I saying we? It's your job, E. J. since you're the briefing DT and my second in command."

"Well, lucky old me," I said, sipping my coffee as the sun crested over the crushed cars outside the window.

CHAPTER
6

THE NYPD'S COUNTERTERRORISM BUREAU was extremely impressive. Outside, it looked like a faceless office building in the middle of a crappy industrial neighborhood. Inside, it looked like the set of 24. There were electronic maps, intense-looking cops at glass desks, and more flat-screen TVs than in the new Yankee Stadium. Walking through the center behind my boss, I felt disappointed that we hadn't been able to enter through a trick manhole and down a slide, like James Bond.

I began to realize why there was so much heat on the library threat. The last thing the commissioner wanted was to have his big, new, expensive initiative to protect the city fail in some capacity. The meeting was held in a glass fishbowl conference room next to something called the Global Intelligence Room. I immediately spotted the assistant commissioner and

the Counterterrorism chief. Though they wore similar golfing attire, their physical contrast was pretty
comical. Flaum was tall and thin, while Cardi was
short and stocky. Rocky and Bullwinkle, I thought.
Laurel and Hardy.

Unfortunately, I also spotted Miriam's boss, Mc-
Girth, who, with his puffy, pasty face, looked like a
not-so-cute reincarnation of Tammany Hall's Boss
Tweed. Beside him were Paul from the Bomb Squad
and the two super fit Feds who had been at the library
the day before. Intelligence briefings about the most
recent terrorist bombings across the globe were
stacked at the center of the long table. I took one as I
found a seat.

"Why don't you start with what you've got,
E. J.?" Miriam said the second my ass hit the cus-
hion.

"Uh, sure," I said, giving her a dirty look as I
stood back up. "Basically, sometime yesterday afternoon, a bomb was left in the main reading room at
the main branch of the New York City Public Lib-

rary. It looked like a Macintosh laptop wired with explosives."

"Damn crazies," one of the detectives mumbled. I continued on.

"It was a sophisticated device, capable of killing dozens of people. A cryptic electronic note left on the laptop stated that the device wasn't intended to go off, but the next one would, sworn to it. There were no witnesses, as far as we can tell at this point."

"Jesus Christ," said Chief McGinnis, making a spectacle of himself as usual.

"Who found the device?" asked Flaum, the tall, professional-looking Intel head.

"An NYU student pointed out the unattended laptop to a security guard," Paul said, jumping in. "The guard opened it, saw the message, ordered an evac, and called us."

"Don't they have a security check there?" Cardi said.

"Yeah, some summer kid checks bags," I said, looking at my notes. "But that's just so people don't steal books. Patrons can take laptops in. He said that Apple laptops are all he sees every day."

"What about security cameras?"

"Deactivated due to a huge ongoing reno," I said.

"Any threats from your end that might be relevant to this, Ted?" assistant commissioner Sander Flaum asked the senior FBI rep. The taller of the two Feds shook his head.

"Chatter hasn't increased," he said. "Though Hezbollah likes to use plastique."

"Hezbollah? That is crazy." Or was it?

"You always seem to be in the middle of this kind of crap, Morris," the chop-busting chief of detectives, McGinnis, said. "What's your professional opinion?"

"Actually, my gut says it's a lone nut," I said. "If it were Hezbollah, why not just set it off? An attention-seeking nut with some particularly dangerous mechanical skills seems to be a better fit."

There was a lot of grumbling. The idea that the bomb might not be terrorism wasn't a particularly popular one. After all, if it was just a lone, sick freak, then why were we all here?

"What about the explosive?" the Intel chief said. "It's from overseas. Maybe the whole nutcase note thing is just window dressing in order to get us off balance. Are nuts usually this organized?"

"You'd be surprised," Miriam said.

"If there aren't any objections, I say we keep it in Major Case until further notice," said the Counterterrorism head as he glanced impatiently around the table.

I was thinking about voicing an objection of my own about how I was supposed to be on vacation, until Miriam gave me a look.

"And try to keep your face from appearing on TV, huh, Morris? This is a confidential case," McGirth said as I was leaving. "I know how hard you find that at times."

I was opening my mouth to return a pithy comment when Miriam appeared at my back and ushered me out.

CHAPTER 7

WITH THAT BUREAUCRATIC HURDLE PAIN-fully tripped over, we headed back to Manhattan. Sunday or no Sunday, we needed to go to our squad room on the 11th floor of One Police Plaza in order to put together a Major Case Squad task force on the Lawrence Bomber Case, as we were now calling it.

I followed Miriam's Impala through Queens and over the Fifty-Ninth Street Bridge. Beyond the windshield, Manhattan's countless windows seemed to stare at me through the bridge's rusty girders. The thought that somebody behind one of them might be meticulously plotting to blow up his fellow human beings right now was not a comforting one. Especially as I hurried across the rattletrap bridge. I received a text on my iPhone as we arrived downtown and snuck in through the back door of HQ.

It was from Emily Parker, an FBI agent I'd worked with on my last case. We'd stayed close since the investigation, so I knew Emily worked a desk at the Bureau's ViCAP, Violent Criminal Appreh-ension Program, which dealt with cheerful things like homicides, sexual assaults, and unidentified human remains.

JUST HEARD ABOUT YOUR PERFORM-ANCE AT NYCT BLUE. DON'T YOU LOVE WORKING WEEKENDS? YOU THE PRIMARY ON THE LIBRARY BOMB THING?

"Talk about a security leak," I thought. How the hell had she found out about our secret meeting this fast on a Sunday? One of her fellow FBI agents at the meeting must have told her, I surmised. She wouldn't actually go out with one of those organic-food-eating geeks, would she?

The fact was, Emily was an attractive lady to whom I'd become quite attached. I would quickly give her some if the time was right and presented itself. I did get to sample her lipstick in the back of an Uber after a case's conclusion one night. I remember its taste fondly. Very fondly, in fact. Too bad that was all I got to taste that night, because I would have definitely been down.

Thinking about it, I suddenly remembered that my baby was home and she was all I needed. Being in a relationship was confusing at times. I stepped onto the elevator while continuing to text.

"You coming or what, text boy?" my boss, Miriam, said as the elevator door opened on eleven. "You're worse than my twelve-year-old."

"Coming, Mother," I said, tucking away my phone before it got confiscated.

● ● ●

Covington's hair was still wet from his shower as he drove his blue Mercedes eastbound out of Manhattan on the Cross Bronx Expressway. Spotting a seagull on the top rail of an exhaust-blackened overpass, he consulted the satellite navigation system screen on the convertible's polished wood dash. Not yet noon, ahead of schedule.

He sipped at a container of black coffee and then slid it back into the cup holder before putting on his turn indicator and easing onto the exit ramp for I-95 north. Minutes later, he pulled off at exit 11 in the northbound lane toward the Pelham section of the Bronx. He drove around for ten minutes before he stopped on a deserted strip of Baychester Avenue.

He sat and stared out at the vista of urban blight. Massive weeds known as ghetto palm trees commanded the cracks in the stained cement sidewalk beside him. In the distance beyond them were buildings, block upon block of massive, ugly brick apartment buildings. The cluster of decrepit high rises was called Co-op City.

From what he'd read, it was the largest single residential development in the United States. Built on a swampy landfill in the 1970s, it was supposed to be the progressive answer to New York City's middle-class housing problem. Instead, like most unfortunate progressive solutions, it had quickly become the problem.

Covington wondered what the urban wasteland had looked like in December of 1975. Worse, he decided with a shake of his head. Enough nonsense, he thought as he drained his cup. He closed his eyes and cleared his mind of everything but the job at hand. He took several slow, deep breaths like an actor waiting backstage.

He was still sitting there doing his breathing exercises when the kitted-out pearl-gray Denali SUV that he was waiting for passed and pulled over a couple of hundred feet ahead.

"What have we here?" Covington said to himself as a young Hispanic woman got out of the truck.

Covington lifted a pair of binoculars off the seat beside him and quickly focused. She was about seventeen or eighteen. She was wearing oversized glasses, a lot of makeup, a scandalously slight yellow bikini top, and denim shorts that were definitely not mother approved. Covington flipped open the manila folder that the binoculars had been sitting on. He glanced at the photograph of the girl, whose name was Aida Morales. It was her, Covington decided. Target confirmed.

The Denali pulled away from the curb, and the girl started walking down the sidewalk toward where Covington sat in the parked car. Covington held back a smile. He couldn't have set up his blind better in a dream. He quickly checked himself in the rearview mirror. He was already wearing the clothes, baggy brown polyester slacks and an even baggier white shirt, butterfly collar buttoned to the neck. He'd padded the shirt with a wadded-up laundry bag to make himself look heavier.

When she arrived at the turn for her building's back entrance, he took out the curly black wig from the paper bag beside him and put it on. He checked himself in the mirror, adjusting the shaggy wig until he was satisfied. She was halfway down the back alley of her building with her all but naked back to him when he started running and yelling.

"Excuse me, miss. Excuse me. Excuse me!" he

cried.

She stopped. She did a double take when she saw the wig. But by then he was too close, and it was too late. Covington pulled the knife from the sheath at his back. It was a shining machete like a military survival knife with a nine-inch blade. Rambo would have been proud.

"Yell and I'll carve your fucking eyes out of your skull," he said as he bunched her bathing suit top at her back like puppet strings.

He hauled her the quick twenty steps to the loading dock by the building's rear even faster than he had visualized. He dragged her into the space between the dock's truck-size garbage compactor and the wall. A little plastic chair sat in the space next to the dock. It was probably where the building's janitor fucked off, he thought.

"Here, have a seat. Get comfy," Covington said, sitting her down on it hard.

Instead of taping her mouth as he had planned, he decided to go ahead and start stabbing her. The garbage stench and the buzzing of the flies were too much for him. The first quick thrust was to her right shoulder. She screamed behind his cupped hand and looked up at the windows and back terraces of her twenty-story building for help. But there were just humming, dripping air conditioners and blank, empty panes of glass all over. They were all alone.

She screamed two more times as Covington removed the knife with a slight tug and then thrust it forward into her left shoulder. She started to weep silently as her blood dripped to the nasty, stained cement.

"There, see?" he said, patting her on the cheek with his free bloody hand. "It's not so bad, right? Almost done, baby. In a minute, we'll both be out of this stinking hole. You're doing so fine."

CHAPTER 8

STILL AT MY DESK LATE SUNDAY AFTERNOON, I'd spent the last two hours scouring the NYPD and FBI databases for any open cases involving the name Lawrence. Though there were quite a few, not one of them seemed to have anything to do with explosives or serial bombings. My eyes felt like blown fuses after I'd sifted through case after irrelevant case.

I glanced up from my computer at the cartoon on the wall of my cubicle, where two cops were arresting a guy next to a dead Pillsbury Doughboy. "His fingerprints match the one on the victim's belly," one of the cops was saying.

If only I could catch a slam dunk like that, I thought, groaning as I rubbed my tired, nonsmiling Irish eyes with the heels of my hands. Scattered around the bullpen behind me, half a dozen other Major Case detectives were running down the lead on the European explosive and questioning potential witnesses and library staff.

So far, just like me, they had complied exactly squat. Without witnesses or likely suspects to connect to the disturbing incident, I was betting it was going to stay that way. At least until our unknown subject struck again. Which was about as depressing as it was gut churning.

It was dark when I finally clocked out and drove home. Fortunately, most of the traffic was in the opposite lane, heading back into the city from Long Island, so I made decent time for a change. My family had quite a surprise for me, as it turned out. It started innocently enough. Jake was sitting by himself in the otherwise empty family room when I opened the front door.

"Hey, lil dude. Where is everyone?"

"Finally," Jake said, putting down the deck of cards he was playing with. He lifted up my swim trunks sitting on the couch beside him and tossed them at me. He stood and folded his arms.

"You need to put them on and follow me," he said cryptically.

"Where?" I said.

"No questions," Jake replied.

My family was nuttier than I was, I thought, after I got changed and let Jake lead me down the two blocks toward the dark beach. Down toward the water's edge, I saw a crowd beside a bonfire. Music was playing loudly.

"Surprise!" everyone yelled as I stepped toward them.

I staggered over, unable to believe it. A few of my guys were there from Philadelphia. They'd brought out the grill, and I could smell ribs smoking. A tub of ice and drinks and a tray of s'mores sat on a blanket. A Morris beach party was in full swing.

"What the heck is this? It isn't my birthday yet."

"Since you couldn't be here for a day on the beach," Amy said, stepping out of the shadows and handing me a can of soda, "we thought you might like a night at it. It was all the kids' idea."

"Wow," I said. "What are y'all doing here?" I asked, talking to Symira, who had come with her new boyfriend, and Trevor, who had come with his wife. I used to work with them in Philly.

"We just wanted to come see this beach house you were renting and get some of that beach life." Sonya smiled.

"We love you, Dad," Shayana said, dropping a plastic lei around my neck and giving me a kiss. "Is that so surprising?"

"Oh, yes, Dad. We love you so much," said Anima, tossing a soaking-wet Nerf ball at me. I even managed to catch it without spilling a drop of soda.

After a few more sodas and some food, I was ready to get in the water. I gathered everyone up and drew a line in the sand with the heel of my bare foot.

"Okay. On your mark, get set . . ."

They were already bolting, the little cheating stinkers, and I hit the ocean a second behind them. I collided with the water face-first, a nail bomb of salt and cold exploding through my skull. Damn, I needed this. My familia was awesome. I was so lucky. We all were.

I let the water knock me silly, then got up and threw someone on my shoulders and waited for the next dark wave. The only light we had was from the moon illuminating the water. Everyone was screaming and laughing like the kids they were. I stared up at the night sky, freezing and having an absolute ball. There was a roar, and another wave came straight at us. We howled as if to scare it away, but it was having none of it. It kept on coming.

"Hold on tight!" I screamed as a tiny sticky finger held on to my bald head. I got to enjoy all this fun with my kids and my friends.

CHAPTER 9

IT WAS DARK WHEN COVINGTON PULLED the Mercedes under the cold, garish lights of a BP gas station at Tenth Avenue and Thirty-Sixth Street back in Manhattan. He'd bagged his bloody clothes and changed back into jeans and a T-shirt immediately after the stabbing. Directly from the scene, he'd driven over the Throgs Neck Bridge, where he'd tossed everything, including the knife and the wig. For the past several hours, he'd been driving around the five boroughs, winding down, blowing off steam, and as always, thinking and planning. He actually did some of his best thinking behind the wheel.

He'd pulled over now not just to fill his tank, but because his braced left knee was starting its all-too-familiar whine. Gritting his teeth at the pain, Covington popped the gas cap and dragged himself up and out of the car, rubbing his leg. He dry swallowed a Percocet, or vitamin P, as he liked to call it, as he filled the tank.

Twenty minutes later, he was piloting the convertible uptown near Columbia University in the Morningside Heights neighborhood. He went west and found meandering Riverside Drive, perhaps the coolest street in Manhattan. He passed Grant's Tomb, all lit up, its bright white Greek columns and rotunda pale against the indigo summer night sky.

He smiled as he cruised Riverside Drive's elegant curves. He had a lot to smile about. Beautiful architecture on his right, dark water on his left, Percocet in his bloodstream. He started blowing some red lights just for the heck of it, cutting people off, putting Stuttgart's latest V8 incarnation through its paces.

He really couldn't get enough of his new $100-,000 toy. Its brute propulsion off the line. How low it squatted in the serpentine curves. Tired of screwing around, Covington picked it up. Slaloming taxis, he hit the esplanade at 125th doing a suicidal eighty.

When he spotted the full moon over the Hudson, he actually howled at it. Then he thought of something. Why not? He suddenly sat up on the seat and drove with his feet the way Jack Nicholson did in a movie he saw once. Wind in his face, holy madness roaring through his skull, Covington sat high up above the windshield, his bare feet on the wheel, arms folded like a genie riding a magic carpet. A woman in a car he flew past started honking her horn. He honked back with his foot.

"Nicholson wished he had balls as big as mine," Covington thought. He really did feel good. Alive for the first time in years, which was ironic since he'd probably be dead as old Ulysses S. back there in a week's time. All in Lawrence's honor, of course. Covington howled again as he dropped back down into his seat and pounded the sports car's engineered accelerator into the floor.

•　•　•

A silver Bentley Arnage with a Union Jack bumper sticker pulled away from the hunter green awning as Covington came hobbling up Seventy-Seventh Street with the cane he kept in the Mercedes trunk. When he entered the birds-eyed lobby, he saw the Sunday doorman packed down with Brickman's Coach Leather bags. His name was Tony, or at least that was what he said it was. His real name was probably something stupid.

"Welcome to New York," Covington thought with a grin, "where Albanians want to be Italians, Jews want to be WASPs, and the mayor wants to be emperor for life."

"Mr. Covington, yes, please," Tony said. "If you give me a moment, I'll press the elevator door button for you."

He was actually serious. Literally lifting a finger was considered quite gauche by some of the building's more obnoxious residents.

"I got this one, Tony," Covington said, pressing the button himself to open it. "Call it an early

Christmas tip."

On the top floor, the mahogany-paneled elevator opened onto a high coffered ceiling hallway. The single door at the end of it led to Covington's penthouse. Brickman had made a discreet and quite handsome offer for it several years before. But some things, like seven thousand multilevel square feet overlooking Central Park, even a billionaire's money couldn't buy.

As he always did once inside the front door, Covington paused with reverence before the two items in the foyer. To the left on a built-in marble shelf sat a dark lacquer jug of Vienna porcelain, a near flawless example of Louis XV-style chinoiserie. Standing before them, Covington felt the beauty and sanctuary of his home descend upon him like a balm. Some would say the old, dark apartment could probably use a remod, but the paneled dusty hallways made him feel like he was living inside an old painting.

This place had been built at a time when there

was still a natural aristocracy, respect for rank and privilege and passion and talent. An urge to ascend. He felt like there were ghosts there in the house that would welcome him home. He decided to draw himself a bath. Covington particularly loved being there in the wintertime. When there was snow on the balcony, he'd open the doors and have the fire roaring as he lay covered in bubbles, looking out at the lights.

He opened the doors before he disrobed and lowered himself slowly into the hot tub. He floated on his back, resting while staring out at the city lights, yellow and white, across the dark sea of trees. Tomorrow he planned on kicking it up to levels unknown, to borrow the words of some obnoxious compared with what people would wake up to tomorrow morning. Tomorrow was going to be one hell of a day.

CHAPTER 10

WAY PAST ALL OUR BEDTIMES AND LOVING it, the kids and I were soaked to the skin and shivering around the bonfire. I heard Seamus clear his throat to tell one of his famous ghost stories. I remembered them from when I was a kid. I mean, anyone can scare a little child. Few can introduce them to cosmic horror.

"Make it a PG tale, huh, Padre?" I said, taking him aside. "I don't want the kids to have nightmares, or me either."

"Fine, fine. I'll water it down, party pooper," Seamus grumbled.

"E. J.?" Amy whispered to me. "Would you help me get some more soda?"

She didn't even make a pretense of heading toward the house. We walked north along the dark beach parallel to the waterline. Amy was wearing a new summer dress that I'd never seen before. Over the past two weeks, she'd become quite brown, which made her blue eyes pop even paler and prettier than usual. She turned those eyes on me and held them there as we walked, an adorably nervous look on her perfect face.

"E. J.," she said as I followed her on our mystical soda quest.

"Yes, baby?"

"I have a confession to make," she said, stopping by an empty lifeguard chair. "I'm not wearing any panties, and I'm very horny right now."

"I'll forgive you on one condition." I smirked, holding her shoulder. "You have to let me taste it before we go back."

There were no more words spoken as she lifted her dress just above her waist, exposing her bald pussy. I was on my knees with the speed of lightning, with my head buried between her legs. We went at it for quite some time, me giving her head, and then her returning the favor. When I entered her from behind,

I damn near melted from the warmness of her pussy. She always felt so good to me.

It didn't take long before I was shooting my load all inside her. I didn't want to stop, but we had to get back to the party.

"Oh no, we're so busted," Amy said. Everyone was gone and the fire was out.

"Who knows? Maybe we'll be lucky and Seamus's fish monsters got them," I joked.

I knew we were in trouble when we saw Le'Shea and Jake standing in the doorway. They both had this look on their faces as if they were relieved to see us.

"They're coming. They're coming. They're not dead," they chanted, running back into the house.

"Oh, yes, we are," Amy said under her breath as they laughed their way into the house.

"Now, where could the two of you have been all this time?" Seamus said with a stupid grin on his face.

"Yeah, Mom and Dad," Anima said. "Where'd you go to get the sodas? Scranton?"

"There was, uh, none left, so I tried . . . I mean, we, uh, went to the store."

"But it was closed and we walked back," Amy finished quickly.

"But there's a case of Coke right here," Jake said from the kitchen.

"That can't be. I must have missed it, 'cause I looked for it and didn't see it," I said.

"In the fridge?" Anima said.

"Enough questions," I said. "I'm the cop here and the dad, in fact. She's the mother. One more question and we're going to be kicking some tail up in here."

Everyone burst into laughter and giggled. Then Seamus had to open his mouth with something smart as he usually does.

"How about a song? Ready, kids? Hit it."

♪ *E.J. and Amy sitting in a tree. K-I-S-S-I-N-G* ♪ they regaled us. Jake and Anima were the loudest. They were making circles around us, dancing and waving their hands. Me and Amy shook our heads.

"You're all dead, you know that," Amy said, red-faced and unable to contain her laughter.

Me and her chased them all around the cabin, throwing pillows at them. It was fun playing with the kids, not worrying about any cases. Of course that would come to an end though.

CHAPTER
11

IT WAS ALREADY HOT AT SEVEN FIFTEEN IN the morning when Covington downshifted the massive Budget rental box truck with a roar and pulled over onto Lexington Avenue near Forty-Second Street. Even this early on Monday morning, people in office clothes were spilling out of Grand Central Terminal like rats from a burning ship.

He threw the massive truck into park and climbed out, leaving it running. He was wearing a Yankees cap backward, cutoff jeans, construction boots, and yellowish-green cheap CVS shades. A wifebeater and a gold chain with a head of Christ topped off his outer-borough truck driver look.

He made a showy display of dropping the back gate and rattling up the steel shutter before wheeling out the hand truck. On it were three thick plastic-strapped bundles of New York Times newspapers.

He rolled them to the truck's hydraulic ramp and started it humming down.

Weaving around morning commuters on the sidewalk, he quickly navigated the hand truck into the train station. Inside, hundreds of people were crisscrossing through the cathedral-like space, running like kids playing musical chairs to get into place before the Stock Exchange's golden opening bell.

A pudgy cop strapping an M16 yawned as Covington rolled right past him. He dropped his bundles by a crowded stationery store called Best Edition. The short, mahogany-colored Asian guy behind the counter came out of the store with a puzzled look on his face as Covington spun the hand truck around with a squeal.

"More Times?" the little brown guy said. "This is a mistake. I already got my delivery."

"Wha—?" Covington said, throwing up his arms. "You gotta be fucking kidding me. I should have finished my deliveries already. Central just called and said to drop these off. Let me call these jagoffs back. Left my cell phone in the truck. I'll be back in a second."

The Asian guy shook his head at the chest-high stack as Covington quickly rolled the hand truck away. As he passed the cop on his way out, he went into his pocket and slid ballistic ear protectors into his ears. Then he turned into the long Lexington Avenue Corridor exit, took the cell phone from his pocket, and dialed the number for the trigger in the paper-wrapped bomb he'd just planted.

He winced as fifty pounds of plastic explosive detonated with an eardrum-splitting ba-bam! Ten feet from the exit door, a chunk of cream-colored marble the size of a pizza slid past him like a shuffleboard disk. A man's briefcase followed. A cloud of dust and hot smoke followed him out the door into the street.

Outside of Lexington, cars had stopped. On the sidewalk, people were turned toward the station's entrance, arrested in place like figures in a model train display. The hand truck clattered over as Covington rolled it off the curb. Passing the rear of the truck he'd parked, he crossed the street and turned the corner of Forty-Third Street, walking quickly with his head down, the iPhone still in his hand.

When he was halfway up the block, he took a breath and dialed the other mobile phone trigger. The one attached to the incendiary device in the cab of the truck. Someone screamed. When he glanced over his shoulder, a pillar of thick black smoke was billowing up between the office towers.

Instead of creating just a distracting blazing truck, he'd seriously thought about filling the rear of the truck with diesel-soaked ammonium nitrate, like the Oklahoma City bomber did, but in the end he'd decided against it. He chucked the hat and the glasses and the Christ head, feeling unsure for a moment, shaking his head. All in due time, he thought. He glanced back at the ink-black pinwheeling mushroom cloud sailing into the July morning sky as he hit Third Avenue and started walking uptown. The first sirens started in the distance.

He hadn't crossed the line this time, Covington knew. He'd just erased it.

• • •

I got up early the next morning. In the predawn gray, I threw on some flip-flops and biked over to a deli a couple of blocks north of our beach bungalow. After I bought a dozen and a half Kaiser Rolls and two pounds of bacon, I sat with a cup of coffee on a beat-up picnic table in the deli's still-dark parking lot, gazing out at the beach. As the sun came up over the ocean, it reminded me of the summer I was seventeen. A buddy and I pulled a Jack Kerouac and hitchhiked down to the Jersey Shore to visit a girl he knew. My friend cut out with the girl, and I ended up sleeping on the beach. Waking alone to the sound of gulls, I was depressed at first, but then I turned to the water and sat there, wide-eyed and frozen, over- whelmed for the first time by what a flat-out miracle this world could be.

I smiled as I remembered being with my beautiful girl last night. She made my dick hard every time I even thought about her. No wonder I was thinking about my teen years, I thought, finishing the dregs of my tea. The only other person that had come close to making me feel like this was my late wife, Ashley. To this day, she still holds a special place in my heart.

After last night, I certainly felt like I was seventeen all over again. I was definitely acting like a kid. Not a bad thing by any stretch in my book. I highly recommend it. Amy was on the porch waiting for me when I got back to the cabin. I could tell by the look on her face that something was terribly wrong. She had my phone in her hand for some reason. I screeched to a stop and dropped the bike as I bolted up the stairs.

"No! What is it? One of the kids?" I asked, thinking that someone hurt one of them. Amy shook her head.

"The kids are fine, Ernest," he said with a surreal

calm.

Ernest? Shit, this was bad. The last time I remembered her using my government name was the time I forgot her birthday. I noticed that the radio was on in the house behind her. A lot of silence between the announcers's halting words. Amy handed me my vibrating phone. There were fourteen text messages from my boss.

"Morris," I said into it as I watched Amy close her eyes and bless herself.

"Oh, E. J.," my boss, Miriam, said. "You're not going to believe this. A bomb just went off in Grand Central Terminal. Four people are dead, dozens more wounded. A cop is among the dead too, E. J."

I looked up at the pink-and-blue sky, then at Amy, then finally down at the sandy porch floorboards. My morning's peaceful decompressing session was officially over. The big, bad world had come back to get my attention like another chunk of cinder block right through my bay window.

"On my way," head spinning. "Give me an hour."

CHAPTER 12

Inbound Manhattan traffic was lighter than usual due to the heart-stopping news. I'd taken my unmarked Grand Marquis home the day before, and as I got on the LIE, I buried the pin of its speedometer, flashers and siren cranked. Keeping off the crowded police band radio, I blasted Young Thug on my satellite radio. That kind of music seemed extremely appropriate for the world coming apart at the seams.

The Anti-Terror Unit in full force had already set up a checkpoint at the 59th Street Bridge. Instead of stopping, I killed some cones as I put the Marquis on the shoulder and took out my ID and pinned the rookie at the barricade at around forty. There were two more checkpoints, one at Fiftieth and Third and the final one at Forty-Fifth and Lex. Sirens screaming in my ears, I parked behind an ambulance and got out.

Behind steel pedestrian barricades to the south, dozens of firefighters and cops were running around in all directions. I walked to take my place among them, shaking my head. When I arrived at the corner and saw the flame-gutted rental truck, I just stood gaping. I spotted Bomb Squad chief Jones through a debris-covered lobby. It looked like a cave-in had happened.

One of the fire chiefs at the blast site's command center made me put on some Tyvek and a full-face air mask before letting me through.

"Guess our friend wasn't lying about the next one," Jones said. "Looks like the same plastique that we found at the library."

He smiled, but I could see the frozen rage in his eyes. He was angry. We all were. Even through the filters of the mask, I could smell death—earth and concrete dust and scorched metal. There was no predicting what would happen next. The rest of the day was as hellacious as any in my career. That morning, I helped an EMT dig out the body of an old, tiny homeless man who'd been buried under the collapsed corridor.

When I went to grab his leg to put him in the body bag, I almost collapsed when his leg separated freely from his body. In fact, all of his limbs had been dismembered by the bomb's shockwave. We had to bag him in parts like a quartered chicken. If that wasn't stressful enough, I spent the afternoon in the on-site morgue with the medical examiner, compiling a list of the dead. The morgue was set up in the Campbell Apartment, an upscale cocktail bar and lounge, and there was something very wrong about seeing covered bodies laid out in rows under a sparkling chandelier.

The worst part was when the slain police officer was brought in. In a private ceremony, the waiting family members were handed his personal effects. Hearing the sobbing moans, I had to get out of there. I walked out and headed down one of Grand Central's deserted tracks. I peered into the darkness at its end for a few minutes, tears stinging in my eyes.

Then I wiped my eyes, walked back, and got back to work.

I met Miriam that afternoon at the Emergency Operations trailer set up by the main entrance of Grand Central on Forty-Second Street. I spotted a horde of media cordoned off on the south side of the street by the overpass behind barricades. National this time. Global newsies would be showing up pretty soon to get their goddamn sound bites from this hellhole.

"We got Verizon pulling recs of the nearest cell sites to see if it was some kind of mobile trigger," Miriam said to me. "The rest of our guys are getting the security tapes from the nearest stores up and down the block. Preliminary witnesses said a large box truck pulled up around seven. A homeless guy sleeping in the ATM alcove in the bank across the street said he looked out and saw a guy pushing a hand truck with something on it before the first explosion."

Miriam paused, staring at me funny before she

pulled me closer so no one else could hear what she was about to say.

"Not only that, E. J. You need to know something else. A letter came to the squad this morning. It was addressed to you. I had them X-ray it before they opened it. It was a typed message. It had today's date along with two words: 'For Lawrence.'"

I closed my eyes, the hair standing up on the back of my neck. Addressed to me?

"For Lawrence?" I said. "What the hell? I mean, give me a break. This is insane. There's no rationale, no demand for ransom. Why was it addressed to me?"

Miriam shrugged her shoulders as Intelligence Chief Flaum came out of the trailer.

"ATF is flying in their guys as we speak to help identify the explosive," he said. "You still think we have a single actor, E. J.? Could that be possible? One person have caused all this?"

Before I could answer, the mayor came out of the trailer, flanked by the police and fire commissioners.

"Good morning, everyone," the mayor said into a microphone. "I'm sorry to have to address you all on this sad, sad day in our city's history."

"Not as sorry as I am," I thought, blinking at the packs of popping flashbulbs. Around four o'clock, I was at Bellevue Hospital, having just interviewed an old Chinese woman who'd lost one of her eyes in the blast, when my cell rang.

"E. J., I hate to tell you this," Amy said. "With everything going on, I know it's not the right time, but—"

"What, Amy?" I barked.

"Everyone's okay, but we're at the hospital. St. John's Episcopal."

I put down the phone for a minute. I took a deep breath. Another hospital? Another problem? This was getting ridiculous.

"Tell me what happened."

"It's Jake. He got into a fight with that Flaherty kid. He got five stitches in his chin, but he's fine. Really he is, E. J. Please don't worry. How is it down there? You must be going through hell."

"It's not that bad," I lied. "I'm actually leaving now. I'm on my way."

Even though Jake wasn't really my son, he was my son. We were a family, and whatever happened to him, happened to all of us. This shit had gone too far now.

CHAPTER 13

ANGRY, DIRTY, AND EMOTIONALLY HOLLOW

I parked in my driveway and sat for a moment. I smelled my hands. I'd scrubbed them at the hospital, but they still smelled like burnt metal and death. I poured another squirt of hand sanitizer into them and rubbed until they hurt. Then I stumbled out and up the porch steps and through the front door.

The dining room table was packed full of my family having dinner. It was silent as a graveyard as I came through the kitchen door. I stepped down to the end of the table and checked out Jake's chin. While I was carrying out the dead, some sick kid had savagely beaten up my stepson. This was my sanctuary, and even this was under siege. Nowhere was safe anymore.

"What happened, guys?"

"We were just playing basketball at the court by

the beach," Jake said. "Then that Flaherty kid came with his older friends. They took the ball, and when we tried to get it back, they started punching."

"Okay, guys. I know you're upset, but we're going to have to try to get through this the best we can," I said with a strained smile. "The good news is that everyone is going to be okay, right?"

"You can call this okay?" Anima said, pointing at Jake's chin. She made Jake open his mouth to show me his chipped tooth.

"Dad, you're a cop. Can't you just arrest this punk?" Le'Shea wanted to know.

"It's not that simple," I said, my voice calm and a convincing fake smile plastered on my face. "There's witnesses and police reports and other adult stuff you guys shouldn't worry about. I'll take care of this. Now, until then, I want everyone to lay low. Stick around the cabin. Maybe even stay away from the beach for a few days."

"A few days? But this is our vacation," Shayana chimed in.

"Yeah, our beach vacation," Anima stated.

"Come on, y'all, listen to your father," Amy said, helping me out.

"Yeah, so what your saying is turn the other cheek on this?" Le'Shea said. She was madder than Jake was.

"That's exactly what I'm saying," Amy said.

"Yeah," Jake said. "So the next time I get socked, the first stitches don't get reopened."

Jake was right. We were getting our asses kicked, and I was too drained to come up with some good bullshit to bluff them that everything was fine. That's when Shayana started crying from the other end of the other table.

"I want to go home," Shayana said.

"I don't like it here anymore," Anima added. "I'm with my little sister. I don't want Jake to be hurt, Daddy. Let's go to Aunt Kimmy's for the rest of our vacation."

Aunt Kimmy lived in Scranton, Pennsylvania, where she and Uncle Lydon owned a mind-blowing, fabulous restaurant called Levels Bistro. We had vacationed that way before moving out to New York, the previous summer.

"Girls, look at me. No one's going to get hurt again, and we can still have fun. I really will take care of this. I promise."

They smiled. Small smiles, but smiles nonetheless. I was happy to get that. I couldn't let them down, I thought. No excuses. New York City under attack or not, I'd have to think of something. But what?

• • •

It was dark when Covington crossed the Whitestone Bridge. He buzzed up the hardtop as he pulled the Mercedes convertible off 678 onto Northern Boulevard in Flushing, Queens. Traffic, crummy airports, an even crummier baseball team. Was there anything that didn't suck about Queens?

He slowly cruised around the grid of streets, trying not to get lost. It wasn't easy with all the small, tidy houses and low apartment buildings set in neat, boring rows everywhere he looked. Thank God for the car's navigation system. After five minutes, he finally stopped and pulled over behind a parked handicapped bus.

It was near a wooded service road alongside the Cross Island Parkway. He turned the Mercedes engine off but left the radio on. He listened to a talk show for a bit, then found a soothing Brahms concerto. When it was over, he sat silently in the darkness. Just sitting there waiting was torture when there was still so much to do.

He'd seriously debated contracting this part out, but in the end he had decided against it. Every small thing was part of the effort, he reminded himself. Even Michelangelo, when painting the Sistine Chapel, built the scaffolds himself and mixed his own paint.

It was almost half an hour later when a new Toyota Camry passed him and turned off the road onto the scheduled lover's lane that ran up the wooded hill alongside an electrical tower cutout. He waited ten minutes to let them get going. Then he slipped on his trusty surgical gloves, got out his new black, curly wig, and grabbed the sack.

Fireflies flickered among the weeds and wildflowers as he stepped up the muggy deserted stretch of service road. It could have been upstate Vermont but for the massive electrical pylon that looked like an ugly, sloppy black stitch across the face of midnight blue sky at the top of the hill.

Even though the parked Toyota's lights were off, Covington caught a lot of motion behind the car's steamed windows as he approached. As the Toyota was rocking back and forth, Covington removed the heavy gun from the paper sack. He arrived at the passenger side window and tapped the snub-nosed chunky .44 Bulldog against the glass. Clink, clink.

"Knock, knock," he said.

They were both in the lowered passenger bucket seat. The beautiful young lady saw him first over the guy's shoulder. She was pretty, a creamy-skinned redhead. Covington took a few steps back in the darkness as she started to scream. As the man struggled to pull up his pants, Covington walked around the rear of the car to the driver's side and got ready.

The Weaver shooting stance he adopted was textbook, two hands extended, elbows firm but not locked, weight evenly distributed on the balls of his feet. When the guy finally sat up, the Bulldog was leveled exactly at his ear. The two huge booms and enormous recoil of the powerful gun were quite surprising after the light, smooth trigger pull.

The driver-side window blew in, and so did most of the horny middle-aged guy's head. The girl in the passenger seat was splattered with blood and brain matter, and her sobbing scream rose in pitch. With the elbow of his shirtsleeve, Covington wiped cordite and sweat out of his eyes. He lowered the heavy revolver and calmly walked around the front of the car back to the passenger side. In situations like this, you had to stay focused, slow everything down.

The woman was trying to climb over her dead lover when he arrived at the other side of the car. Covington took up the position again and waited until she turned. Two more dynamite-detonating booms sounded out as he grouped two .44 Bulldog rounds into her pale forehead. Then there was silence, Covington thought, listening.

Recoil tingling his fingers, he dropped the gun back into the paper sack and retrieved the envelope from his pocket. He flicked the envelope through the shattered window. There was something typed across the front of it.

E. J. MORRIS NYPD. Humming the concerto he'd just been listening to, Covington tugged at a rubber glove with his teeth as he hurried back down the hill toward his car.

CHAPTER 14

"GOING OUT FOR ICE CREAM," I SAID, getting up from the game of Trivial Pursuit we started playing after dinner.

Amy gave me a quizzical look as I was leaving. Her concern only seemed to increase when I gave her a thumbs-up on the way out the screen door. But instead of getting ice cream, I hopped into the Marquis and called into my squad to get the address for the Flaherty family in Breezy Point. Was that a little crazy? It was, but then again, so was I by that point.

Their house was on the Rockaway Inlet side of the Point about ten blocks away. I drove straight there. They really did have a pit bull chained in their front yard. It went mad as I stepped out of my car and made my way up the rickety steps. It wasn't madder than me though. I actually smiled at it. After today and everything I had seen, I was in a man-bites-dog sort of mood. I pounded on the door.

"Oh, this better be good," said the bald guy who answered it. Now, I was bald by choice, but this guy was bald because he had to be.

The guy was big. He was also shirtless and in damn good shape, I could see: huge bowling-ball shoulders, six-pack abs, prison yard pumped. There was another man, just as big and mean looking and covered in tattoos, standing behind him. I should have been cautious then. I knew a violent criminal mobster asshole when I saw one. But I guess I was through giving a shit for the day.

"You Flaherty?" I said.

"Yeah. Who the fuck are you?"

"My name's Morris. You have a kid?"

"I got five of 'em at least. Which one we talking about here?"

"Fat, freckles, about sixteen. Did I say fat?"

"You talking about my Seany? What's up?"

"Yeah, well your Seany split my son's chin open

today is what's up," I said, staring into Flaherty's soulless doll's eyes. "He had to go to the hospital."

"That can't be right," the man said, stone-faced. He smiled coldly. "We went fishing today, all day. Hey, Billy, remember when Sean caught that blowfish today?"

"Oh, yeah," the thug behind him said with a guffaw. "Blowfish. That was the puffy balloon thing, right? That shit was funny."

"See. Guess you made a mistake," Flaherty senior said. "Wait a second. Morris. I know you. You got four crumb crunchers, right? You're a cop, too. Look, Billy, it's the OctoCop in the flesh."

"I do have a gun," I said with a grin. "You want me to show it to you?"

I really did feel like showing it to him. In fact, I actually felt like giving him a taste of my Glock.

"I know what they look like, but thanks anyway," Flaherty said, cold as ice. "If you don't mind, though, I'd like to get back to the ballgame. The Mets might even win one for a change. Have a nice night,

Officer."

That's when he slammed the door in my face. I felt like kicking it in. The pit was in a frenzy, so was I. Even in my stress-induced hysteria, I knew that wasn't a good idea. I chose to retreat. An empty Miller High Life can landed beside me as I was coming down the steps. Young Flaherty himself waved to me from the rattletrap's second-story window.

"Gee, Officer, I apologize. Must have slipped out of my hand."

Even over the dog's apoplexy, I heard raucous laughter from inside. Death all day and ridicule for dessert, what a day. I crushed the can and hit the stairs before I could take my gun out.

• • •

Returning to the house with a full head of steam, I decided I needed some alone time. Wanting to make it both relaxing and constructive, I opted for doing what any angry, overworked cop in my situation would do. Inside the garbage, I tossed down some old newspaper on a workbench and began field stripping my Glock 21.

For half an hour, I went to town, cleaning the barrel and slide until everything was shipshape and shining like a brand-new penny. I'm not proud to admit that as I went through the motions meticulously, some thoughts went through my mind concerning certain Breezy Point residents. As I reloaded the semi-auto's magazine and slapped it home with a well-oiled snick, I made a mental note to set up a confession the next time I saw Seamus.

While I was standing there pondering my next move, I heard steps on the porch and the doorbell ring.

"Hey, is Anima around?" a voice called out.

That voice belonged to Joe somebody from up the block who kept coming around because he had a crush on Anima.

"Hey, Joe," I overheard Anima say a second later.

"Do you and Jake and your other sisters want to play roundup again?" the sly Breezy Point Romeo wanted to know.

"Can't tonight, Joe, but I'll text you tomorrow, okay?" Anima said curtly before letting the door close in his face with a bang.

That was odd, I thought, heading outside and up the porch steps after Joe left. I knew my stepdaughter had a bit of a crush on the kid as well. What was up? I figured it out when I saw Anima through the front window. She was sitting on the couch, laughing, painting Shayana's toenails as Le'Shea waited her turn. I spotted Amy sitting in the recliner with cucumber slices over her eyes.

I stood there shaking my head, amazed. Anima knew how upset this whole Flaherty thing had made her sisters, so she had scratched her plans to comfort them with some sister spa time. Amy was a bonus to their session because she was there. While I was itching to crack someone's face, Anima was stepping in, stepping up.

I sat outside on the porch, thinking about everything that had been happening these last few days. All I wanted to do was have a nice vacation with my family, and instead, I was stuck with a bomber and a family that liked bullying others.

Almost an hour later, Amy came out. She frowned at my sad, self-pitying ass as she sat down beside me.

"And how are the Flahertys?" she asked.

I looked at her, about to deny my visit to the neighbors. Then I cracked a tiny smile.

"Bad news, Amy," I said, looking off down the sandy lane, "which is about par for the course lately, isn't it? For this vacation. This city. This planet."

She wisely went back inside and left me alone with my black mood. When my work phone rang a half hour later with my boss's cell number on display, I seriously thought about throwing it as hard as I could off the porch. Maybe taking a couple of potshots at it before it landed, my own personal Breezy Point clay shoot. Then I remembered what my stepson Jake had said two days before. Who was I kidding? Vacations were for real people. I was a cop.

"This is Morris," I said into the phone with a grim smile. "Gimme a crime scene."

"Coming right up," Miriam said.

CHAPTER
15

AS I DROVE THROUGH QUEENS TWENTY minutes later, I thought about a documentary I once saw on Hulu about the annual NYPD Finest versus the FDNY Bravest football game. At halftime, with the score tied, the firemen's locker room was about what you'd expect: upbeat, healthy-looking players and coaches encouraging one another. The NYPD locker room, on the other hand, was about as cheerful as the visitor's room at Rikers. In place of a traditionnal pep talk, raging cops opted for screaming horrendous obscenities at one another and punching the lockers like violent mental patients.

No doubt about it, we're a funny bunch. "Not funny ha-ha, either," I thought as I arrived at the latest atrocity, a murder scene along an industrial service road in Flushing. I was a little fuzzy as to why I, of all people, needed to come to this godforsaken place in the middle of the night when I was already up to my eyeballs in the bombing case. But I was pretty sure I was about to find out.

Besides an electrical pylon at the top of the access road, half a dozen detectives and uniforms were taking pictures and kicking through the weeds, accompanied by police band radio chatter. In the far distance behind them, cars continued zipping by on the lit-up Whitestone and Throne Neck Bridges. With the red-and-blue police strobes skipping through the trees, there was something bucolic, almost peaceful about the whole scene. Too bad peace wasn't my business. Definitely not tonight.

A short, immaculately dressed Filipino detective from the 109th Precinct pulled off a surgical glove and introduced himself to me as Andy Hunt while I was signing the homicide scene log. The death scene Hunt guided me to was a new Toyota Camry with a nice tan leather interior. "Formerly nice," I corrected myself as I stepped up to the driver's-side open door and saw the ruined bodies.

A middle-aged man and a younger woman leaned shoulder to shoulder in the center of the car, both shot twice in the head with a large-caliber gun. Green beads of shattered auto glass covered both bodies. I waved away a fly, staring at the horrible constellation of dried blood spray stuck to the dash.

"The male victim is one Eugene Keating. He was a professor at Hofstra, taught international energy policy, whatever the hell that is," Detective Hunt said, tossing his Tiffany-blue silk tie over his shoulder to protect it as he leaned in over the victims.

"The redhead is Karen Lang, one of his graduate students. Maybe they were testing the carbon output on this electrical cutout, but I have my doubts, considering her panties on the floor there. What really sucks is that Keating has two kids and his pregnant professor wife is due for a C-section in two days. Guess she'll have to call a cab to the hospital now, huh?"

"I don't understand though," I said, resisting the urge to pull down the poor female victim's bunched up T-shirt. "Why does anyone think this tower has something to do with today's bombing?"

Hunt gave me an extra-grim look. Then he moved the light onto something white that was sitting in the dead man's lap. It was an envelope with something typed across the front of it. I squatted down to get a better look. You're not supposed to let the job get inside you, but I have to admit that when I read my name on the envelope, I absolutely panicked. I froze from head to toe as if someone had just pressed an invisible gun to my head.

After a few minutes, I shrugged off my heebie-jeebies and decided to go ahead and open it. With thoughts of Ted Kaczynski, the Unabomber, dancing in my head, I retrieved the envelope with the pliers of Hunt's multi-tool. I borrowed a folding knife from one of the uniforms and slit the envelope open on the hood of the nearest cruiser.

If I thought opening the letter was a hair-raising experience, it couldn't hold a candle to what it said on the plain sheet of white paper inside:

Dear Detective E. J. Morris:

I am deeply hurt by your calling
me a woman hater. I am not. But I
am a monster. I am better than
you think. I am the secret in the dark.
Just call me the Grim Reaper.

CHAPTER 16

WEARING A PINK BANANA REPUBLIC BUT-ton down shirt, khakis, and a pair of loafers, Covington whistled as he carried a brimming tray of Starbucks coffees south down Fifth Avenue with the rest of the early morning commuters. Shaved and gelled to a high-gloss metrosexual sheen, he even had a corporate ID badge with the improbable name Cory Gonzalez emblazoned across it like a hello sticker. In this elitist venue of publishing houses and television company officers that was the Rockefeller Center business district, his just-so-casual creative-type office-worker look was better camouflage than a sniper's ghillie suit.

Pounding hammers and clicking socket wrenches and muffled shouts rang off the granite walls as he turned right down Rockefeller Center's east concourse. Covington almost tripped over a gray-haired, pot-bellied roadie on his knees who was taping down some cables.

Covington knew that the stage was being erected for the Today show's outdoor summer concert series, to be broadcast at 8:15 this morning. The musical artist, a young man by the ponderous name of Showtime, was going to perform his hit song, "Ride wit Me."

Already people had arrived for the event. Faces painted, holding signs, they were anticipating a fun morning of dancing and singing along with the ex-drug-dealing rapper as he performed his soulful joy of public sexual activity. Covington had a catchphrase for today's youth that he was waiting for the ad firms to pick up on. First, you had Generation X, then Generation Y. Now welcome ye, one and sundry, I introduce Degeneration 1.

Anyone who didn't see the cheerful acceptance of this gutter dirt by the general public, and especially by the young, as a sign of the coming new Dark Ages lacked a working mind or was madder than

Alice's Hatter.

Once upon a time Rome fell. Now it was our turn. The Show was here to provide the background music. Covington passed a group of giggling high school girls. "Enjoy the bottom feeding," he thought as he carefully left one of his coffees on the ledge of a planter he passed. Without looking back, he stepped out onto Sixth Avenue and hailed a taxi.

● ● ●

It was almost 8:00 a.m. by the time Covington got back to his apartment. Inside the high, dim alcove, he actually genuflected before Salvador Dali's first painting, praying to the great Spaniard for help and strength.

He remembered a quote from the Master. "At the age of six, I wanted to be a cook. At seven, I wanted to be Napoleon, and my ambition has been growing steadily ever since."

Covington stood, smiling. Each moment, each breath, came that much sweeter the closer he approached his death. In the beginning, he had been afraid when he thought about how things would turn out. Now he saw that bit all made perfect sense. He was glad.

In the apartment's imposing library, Covington slowly removed all of his clothing. He lifted the remote control and stood before the massive screen of the $50,000 103-inch Zenith plasma TV. He glanced at the butter-soft leather recliner where he'd sat to watch all his favorite movies, but he didn't sit down. For this, he preferred to stand.

He clicked on the set. There was a commercial for a feminine product, and then Matt Lauer filled the wall of the room.

"Without further ado," Lauer said, "let's cut to the Plaza and The Show."

A young black man in a full-out orange prison jumpsuit covered in gold chains winked from the screen.

Behind him, a retinue of other prison suited young male and female backup singers and dancers of every race was standing, still as Buckingham Palace guards, waiting for the first drop of bass to start kicking it freestyle.

Many of the young people in the crowd had cell phones in their hands and were recording the momentous occasion. Covington lifted his own phone, but it wasn't to take a picture. It was to paint his own. He pressed the speed dial.

"And one, two," The Show said.

"Show's over," Covington said.

There was a flush of light. A startling blast of sound followed by a long, cracking echo. The Show stood there, microphone to his gaping mouth, as the camera panned over his shoulder onto a plume of smoke. In 1080 HD with Dolby surround, Covington was psyched. He changed to channel 2. CBS's Early Show was on. The host, some slutty-looking bimbo, was grilling fish out on the studio's Fifty-Ninth and Fifth Avenue plaza with none other than celebrity chef John Katz.

"Ja, you see? Ja," John said.

"Ja, Volfie, I see, I see," Covington said as he thumbed another speed dial button for the second device he'd planted next to the corner garbage can at the chef's back.

Another explosion, even louder than the first, happened immediately. Someone started screaming.

"That's what you get," Covington chided, clicking over to ABC.

Diane Sawyer was interviewing a sportswriter who was shilling his latest vapid tear-jerking bestseller. They were outside on one of ABC's Times Square Studio's roof plazas.

"Tell me, where do you get your ideas?" Diane wanted to know.

"On second thought, don't," Covington said as he dialed the third bomb that he'd left in the center of Times Square, down on the street beneath her.

The sound was softer, which made sense due to the elevation, Covington thought, looking down at the Oriental carpet. Had there been a little glass shattering in that one?

He nodded with a grin. Indeed, there had been. Exceptional! Satisfied, he shut off the massive set. Watching the ensuing chaos would prove what? People were afraid of explosives? He knew that already, better than most. Now it was time to rest up before lunch.

He was actually pretty proud of the bombs. They were simple, Venti-size sticks of dynamite attached to a Wi-Fi antenna wired to a watch battery with a thin piece of detcord for the boost. Not huge, but just big enough to make everybody scared shitless. Big enough to make everyone start to carefully ponder their next step. With high explosives, it was all about the real estate. Location, location, location.

He went into his bathroom and opened the tap. He dropped in the bubble soap and bath crystals and lit some candles. On the sound system, he put on a new CD that he'd gotten at Bed Bath & Beyond. He popped a couple of vitamin P-is-for-Percocets and slid into the warm water as a woman's voice rang like an angel's off the glowing white Tyrolean marble walls.

"Who can say where the road flows?" Covington sang along. He closed his eyes and drifted off to sleep.

CHAPTER 17

I was sitting at the table eating doughnuts and drinking milk with Shayana and Anima, when someone made the mistake of putting on the television.

"Dad! Dad! You have to see this!" Le'Shea yelled.

"I'm a cop," I said, calling into the living room. "Don't mess with a cop when he's anywhere near a doughnut."

I winked at Anima and Shayana across the table. They seemed to be in a good mood after having had a good night's sleep. I was hoping that today would be much better than the last couple of days. I was due for a relaxing day.

"But it's another bombing, Dad. At Rockefeller Center. No one died, it says at the bottom of the screen, but a dozen people are in the hospital. The mad bomber strikes again."

Rockefeller Center? This loser didn't quit, did he? Or was it two people? One Grim Reaper copycat and another fool? I didn't even look for my phone. I didn't need my boss to tell me where I needed to be. Running for the shower, I passed Amy coming in with my sandwich.

"I'll need to take that to go."

I took a shower, got dressed, and headed out in a hurry. Pedal to the metal, flashers and siren cranked to full amplification, I plowed a swath through the BQE's left lane that morning. A scraggly red Ford pickup that had missed out on the Cash for Clunkers deal tried to cut in a hundred feet in front of me. His mirrors must have been broken, as well as his ears. I roared up until I was practically in his rusting truck bed before I sent him packing with a fierce barrage of machine-gunning yawps and whoops.

No wonder I was on the warpath. What was happening was beyond incredible. Police presence had been beefed up at all major public places around the city, and still our bomber had managed to set off even more explosives. At the same time as all three network morning shows were being broadcast, no less!

I thought about the crime scene from the night before. I lifted my iPhone as I pounded past a nasty stretch of Queens tract housing and half-finished construction sites. Talking on the phone was beyond stupid and reckless, considering I had my cop car up near the three-digit range, but what was I going to do? Stupid and reckless happened to be my middle and confirmation names this crazy morning. It was time to brainstorm with Emily Parker down at the FBI's Violent Criminal Apprehension Program in Virginia.

"Parker," Emily said.

I quickly told her about the previous night's murder scene and the Grim Reaper letter addressed to me.

"So not only is someone setting off bombs every three seconds, but the Grim Reaper has apparently returned," I said in conclusion. "And to top things off, the only connection between the crimes so far seems to be a desire to correspond with lucky old me."

"You think the three terrorist acts are connected to the Grim Reaper copycat killer?" Emily said. "That is truly bizarre."

That's when I remembered what Anime said as I was leaving. I almost ran off the elevated expressway: "The mad bomber strikes again!"

"Wait! The Mad Bomber. Of course!" I cried. "It isn't a terrorist act, Emily. The bombings are copycats too. There actually was a Mad Bomber who terrorized New York in the '40s or '50s, I think."

"Hold up, E. J. I'm at the computer," Emily said. I could hear her typing.

"My God, E. J., you're right. It's right here on Wikipedia. The guy's name was George Metesky. He was known as the Mad Bomber, and it says here that in the forties and fifties, he planned bombs at New York landmarks. Wait! It says he planted bombs at the Public Library and Grand Central

Terminal."

I shook my head.

"Is that what this is?" I said. "Someone or more than one person is copycatting two famous crime sprees at once?"

"But how?" Emily said, sounding astounded. "Think about the logistics. How could it be coordinated? Four bombings and a double murder in a little over twenty-four hours?"

"Well, from the sophistication of the bombs, we're not dealing with dummies," I said as I fumbled my grip on my phone. I was just able to catch it against my chest.

When I looked back up, I immediately stopped thinking about the case. In fact, my entire brain stopped functioning. Then my lungs. Because around a curve in the expressway, being approached at roughly the speed of light, were three packed lanes of dead stopped traffic.

For a few precious fractions of a second, I did nothing but gape at the frozen red wall of brake lights. Then I did four things pretty much simultan-eously. I screamed, released the phone, let off the gas, and slammed on the brakes. Nothing happened. In fact, the brakes felt suddenly looser than normal. "Are they broken?" I thought, pissed. I knew the car had ABS. It was perhaps the only thing on my shock scrambled mind as I hurtled toward the rapidly approaching rear of a Martz Bus.

I wondered in my panic if I was doing it right. Was I supposed to hold or pump the brakes? I couldn't remember. My fear-locked leg decided for me, keeping the pedal down as far as it would go. The brake pedal gave a couple of hard jerks under my foot and then felt even looser. The line had snapped under the strain, I decided. The steel wall of the bus in my windshield got larger and closer by the millisecond.

It was over, I concluded. I was going to hit it head-on, and it was going to be very bad. That's when a slow-motion, life-flashing-before-your-eyes sensation kicked in. I glanced to my right as I lasered past a white Volkswagen Jetta. The pretty young brunette behind the wheel was putting on mascara. Turning back toward the rear of the bus that I was about to become part of, I wondered if she was the last human face I would ever see.

My last thought as I braced my arms against the steering wheel was of my kids and Amy. How hard and royally shitty it was going to be for them to lose not just their mother, but their careless father as well. I closed my eyes, and the car just stopped.

No skidding, no warning. There was a brief scream of rubber, and it was like God slipped his hand between my car and the bus, and I went from sixty to zero in zero point zero seconds. Too bad I was still moving. My sternum felt like it was hit with an ax handle as my chest bumped my locked shoulder belt. My dropped iPhone catapulted off the passenger seat like an F-14 off a carrier. It ricocheted off the glove box and whizzed past my ear like a bullet.

"Guess I should have bought that merchandise insurance after all," I thought as I sat blinking and shuddering behind the wheel. Was I still alive? I decided to check. I took a sweet drink of oxygen and, like magic, turned it into carbon dioxide. Then I did it again. My heart was still beating too. It felt like it was trying to tear itself out of my chest, but that was neither here nor there. Being alive was fun, I decided.

CHAPTER
18

I WAITED A FEW MORE SECONDS TO SEE IF St. Peter was going to show. When he didn't, I backed away from the rear of the idling bus. Ignoring the dumbstruck looks from my fellow motorists in the other lanes, I reached into the back of the car and retrieved my phone.

The screen was shot, but the phone was actually still working. Miracles were abounding this morning. Since traffic was at a standstill, I decided to call Emily back.

"E. J., what happened?" Emily said when I got her on the phone.

"Oh, nothing," I said, wiping cold sweat out of my eyes with my free palm.

I was going to leave it at that, but then the fear and adrenaline caught up with me, and my hands started to shake so badly, I had to lie the phone down and put it on speaker.

"You sure?"

"Actually, I almost just killed myself, Emily," I told her. "I was flying back into Manhattan and turned a corner, coming within an inch or two of embedding myself in the rear end of a tour bus."

"My God! Are you okay?"

"My hands won't stop shaking," I said. "I thought I'd bought it there for a second, Em."

"Pull over and take some deep breaths E. J. I'm right here with you."

I followed her advice. It wasn't just what she said, but the way she said it. Emily really was a supportive person. I remembered her on our previous case together. How caring she was with one of the young kidnapping victims. She knew when to push and when to hold back. She was a terrific agent and a deeply caring person. She was very attractive too. We kind of fell for each other during the case. Well, I know I fell for her. Too bad I was in a relationship, or else I would have hit that if the chance presented itself.

"E. J.? You still there?"

"Barely," I said. She laughed.

"Well, I for one, am glad your head's still attached to your shoulders. I like the way it thinks. The way it looks isn't that bad either."

"What did she say?" I thought, squirming at the phone. If I didn't know any better, I could have sworn that this beautiful woman was just flirting with me.

"Ah, you're just saying that to keep me from going into shock," I replied.

"That's what friends are for," Emily said. "Actually, they want to send someone from our team up to New York to help you guys out, E. J. I was wondering if you thought it was a good idea if I volunteered?"

I thought about that. It went without saying that her expertise on the case would be invaluable, and it really would be awesome to see her. Maybe we could even fool around a bit. Just as long as she knew that

I was in a relationship and wasn't leaving Amy. Hoping that this wouldn't go south, the next thing I said surprised me.

"Come on up. We need all the help we can get. We need the best people on this. Besides, it would be great to see you."

"Really?" she said.

"Really," I replied, not knowing what the hell I was doing or saying. "Call me as soon as you get up here."

● ● ●

I somehow managed to complete the rest of my commute safely and arrived at the closest bombing scene, at Fifty-Ninth Street and Fifth Avenue, around 9:30 a.m. The area across from the Plaza Hotel and Central Park was usually packed with rich ladies who lunch and tourists looking for overpriced horse-and-buggy rides.

Now an occupying force of assault-rifle-strapping Emergency Service Unit storm troopers had cordoned off the corner, and instead of chipoos peeking from Fendi clutches, bomb-sniffing Labradors were sweeping both sides of the street. I noticed an aggravating CBS News camera aimed directly between my eyes as I came under the crime scene tape in front of the GM Building.

I guess I couldn't complain that the media had already gotten here, since, including ABC and NBC, they seemed to be the targets. As if Tiffany's and the network studios weren't high-profile enough, the world-famous VAO Schwartz toy store sat on the other side of the outdoor space, as well as the funky transparent glass cube of the wild Fifth Avenue sunken Apple store.

I found the Bomb Squad's second-in-command, Brian Dunning, chewing gum as he knelt on the intersection of the southeast corner, in front of a blast-blackened streetlight. At the Grand Central scene, Jones had told me that the blond pock-faced tech was freshly from Iraq, where he'd been part of a very busy army EOD team.

Since it seemed New York was currently at war
as well, I was glad he was on our side. The toppled
garbage can beside him had a hole in its steel mesh
the size of a grapefruit. What looked like tiny pieces
of confetti were scattered on the sidewalk and street
beside it. It reminded me of firecracker paper on the
day after the Fourth of July. I scooped some of it up
to get a better look.

"It's cardboard," Dunning said, standing. "From
a coffee cup, is my guess. Which would blend in
perfectly in a garbage can. You want an IED to
appear totally innocuous."

"Was it plastic explosives, like the last one?" I
said. Dunning smelled the piece of cardboard.

"Dynamite, I'd say off the top of my head. About
a stick or so, I'd guess. Mobile phone trigger with a
fuse-head electric blasting cap packed in a coffee cup
all as neat as you please. This cop-killing freak's got
skills. I'll give him that."

Great, I thought. Our guy was using new
materials. Or maybe not, I thought, letting out a

breath. It could have been someone else catching the heat of the moment and getting in on the act. More questions without any answers, I thought. What else was new? I caught up to my boss, who was talking with a group of shaken-up Early Show staffers.

"No one seems to have seen a thing, E. J.," Miriam said as we walked toward the corner. "They have security out here on the Plaza, of course, but they don't detour pedestrian traffic. Sanitation said they collected this morning at five. Our guy must have dropped the coffee cup sometime after that, probably as he was waiting for the light. This guy's a ghost."

I quickly went over the copycat theory that Emily and I were working on.

"He's not just copying the Grim Reaper," I said. "In the '40s, a disgruntled Con Ed employee named George Metesky planted bombs in the movie theaters and public places. For sixteen years, he set off gunpowder-filled pipe bombs in the same places this guy has hit. The library, Rockefeller Center, Grand

Central. It fits, boss."

She stepped off the sidewalk into the street. We looked down Fifth Avenue at the Empire State Building for a few beats.

"So you're saying that this guy isn't just some regular run-of-the-mill violent psycho?" she said.

I nodded. "I think we have some kind of super-competent and super-loony NYC crime buff out there giving nods to those he admires," I said.

CHAPTER
19

FOR THE REMAINDER OF THE DAY, I VISITED the other crime scenes at Rock Center and Times Square, where I learned absolutely nothing new. No one in Times Square had seen a man dropping a coffee cup, not even the Naked Cowboy. The entire Major Case Squad was going blind reviewing security video footage from surrounding stores and buildings, but so far nothing had made itself evident.

It was the same story for the red-balled forensics test on the letter from the Flushing double murder. There was a brief moment of hope when I learned that the VIN for the truck involved in the Grand Central bombing had been traced. But that hope had been dashed with authority when it turned out that it was a stolen rental truck.

Who steals a rental truck? A psycho was the answer to that one. A very neat and tidy anal psycho.

The worst kind of all, and to top it all off, I still couldn't shake how I'd almost died on the BQE through my own sheer stupidity. It was around ten that night when I got off the exit for Breezy Point. There was no music when I pulled up in front of the Morris beach house. Definitely no drinks outside waiting for me. In fact, all the lights in the house were off. I remembered Amy was at her night class at Columbia. Not good.

Somebody was on the porch. It was my stepson, Jake, pacing back and forth, holding a baseball bat. It didn't look like he was practicing his swing.

"Don't tell me something else happened," I groaned. "Wasn't today any better?"

"No one told you, Dad? Shayana and Anima went out to get ice cream, and a bunch of a-holes threw some eggs at them from a passing car. Not only that, but when Shayana rode her bike back to the store, she came out and found this."

He rolled the bike over and showed me the front tire sliced to ribbons.

"I'm going to kill this kid, Dad. I swear, I'm going to kill him."

"And I'm going to absolve him when he does," Seamus said, stepping onto the porch with a golf club. I let out a breath. Home Insane Home.

"The worst thing," Seamus said, "is that all the fookin' Flahertys go to Sunday mass. Like it's going to keep them out of hell, which it isn't, the little heathens. The host should burn holes in their tongues."

"Enough about going on a warpath, you fighting crazies," I said. "Jake, listen, I know you're mad, but we need to be smart about this. You let this punk bait you, and you'll be the one who gets arrested."

"Maybe we should do what Anima said then, Dad," Jake said, dropping the mangled bike. "Maybe we should just clear out, because this vacation is starting to suck."

I lifted up the bike and carried it off the porch and into the garage. I popped off the tire with a screwdriver and looked through the shelves for a patch kit.

"He's right, you know," Seamus said, coming in as I put rubber cement over the first gash.

"About what?" I asked.

"This vacay is starting to suck. Big time," Seamus said.

● ● ●

Later that night, I sat on the porch swing, having pulled guard duty. I had a plastic cup of orange soda in one hand and Jake's Louisville Slugger in the other. Summer of Love Part 2, this was not.

"Hark, who goes there?" I said as Amy came up the stairs, home from her class.

She was wearing tight jeans with a jazzy leopard-print tank and looking amazing. She made me hard every time I saw her. It didn't matter what she wore. She always looked delicious.

"We're arming ourselves? It's that bad, huh?" Amy said as she shrugged off her laptop bag and sat her spectacular body down beside me. I poured my woman a glass of her favorite wine.

"Worse," I said, handing it to her.

"Are they all asleep?"

"At least pretending to be," I said. "All except the big one."

"Jake?"

"No Father Pain-in-the-Ass. He went out for a few jars, quote unquote, to soothe his troubled mind. Even the saints are hitting the suds tonight," I said, clinking plastic cups.

"Are you any closer to catching the bomber guy?" she asked, kicking off her flats. "Because the people in my class are completely bonkers. Half of them didn't even show up for tonight's test. They told the professor they're too afraid to ride the trains."

"Smart kids," I said. "You might want to follow their example. If the color code thing were still in place, we'd be looking at orange, dark orange."

"I'm a big girl, E. J. I know my way around the city now. I can take care of my own self."

"I know that, but if something happens to you, who's going to take care of me?" I said.

We swung back and forth for a while, talking and having fun. She told me some funny stories about her summer vacations with her family when she was a teenager. Even after the day I'd had, I was actually starting to relax.

"The whole time I was in class, I was thinking about you and my friend here." She rubbed my dick. I was hard as usual.

I don't remember who started kissing whom first, but we were all over each other. The waves were incredibly choppy and loud, making a relentless pounding noise. The first hurricane of the season was heading up the East Coast from Florida, I remembered I'd heard on the radio.

"I think we need to go in the house and take this in the bedroom," I whispered in her ear.

"I'm horny now," Amy moaned, Pulling off her jeans right there on the porch. Of course she was wearing her famous leopard thong. "If you don't want to, just let me know, and I'll go in the house and please myself." I smiled knowing that she wasn't bluffing.

"Stop playing and get your sexy ass over here," I told her, pulling her down on my lap.

I slid her thong to the side and slid right in. Knowing that we only had a few minutes if we didn't want to get caught, we wasted no time. It didn't take long for her to explode; then I followed. The hurricane was slowly passing in the sky according to the DJ on the radio.

That's when I remembered something else. The hurricane wouldn't be the only thing coming up to New York. "Why had I told Emily Parker to come again?" I thought as Amy slid back into her pants. Because she was a competent law enforcement expert? Even I knew that was bull. Emily was cute, and I liked her. But Amy was by far the most beautiful woman I had seen in a long time. Plus, she was all mine.

I was fixing my clothes and smiling at Amy as

she stared at me. She leaned down and gave me some more of her tasty tongue. I pulled her back into my lap.

"Eh-hem," someone yelled.

I don't know who jumped higher, me or Amy. There was a jangle of chains as we almost fell out of the chair. I looked up and saw Seamus.

"And how was your class tonight, Amy? Your art class, that is, if you don't mind me asking?"

"Oh, fine, Seamus. Look at the time. So much to do tomorrow. Goodnight, Seamus," Amy said. "I'll see you when you come to bed, E. J."

"You two better behave yourselves. That could have been the kids coming out here," Seamus said, then headed back in the house. I didn't say a word because I knew he was right.

CHAPTER 20

TO THE CLACK OF KITCHEN PLATES, THE PALE, elegant brunette weaved her way around the dim room's empty linen-covered tables and climbed the little corner stage to reach the ebony Steinway Concert Grand. After a moment, a slow and pretty impressionistic piece began to drift out over the room, Debussy or maybe Ravel.

At the opposite end of the wood-paneled room, Covington nodded with approval. Then he carefully tucked his damask napkin into his shirt, closed his eyes, and inhaled. Invisible ribbons of hunger-inflaming scents from the vicinity of the swinging kitchen door behind him invaded his quivering nostrils. He detected nutty sizzling butters, meat smoke, soups redolent of mushrooms and leeks, decanted vintage wine.

His palate was so sensitive, he felt he could actually distinguish the separate odors dissolving against the postage-stamp-size tissue called the olfactory epithelium, high in his nasal cavity.

"Now, sir?" whispered the bug-eyed tuxedo-clad maître d' at his back.

The arrangement was that only the maître d' could serve or speak to him. Covington never spoke back, but rather indicated his wishes with a series of predetermined head and facial gestures. He had even asked that the shades be drawn to keep the dining space as dark as possible. Covington waited a moment longer, holding in the glorious aromas, a junkie with a hit of crack smoke. Then he gave a subtle nod.

The maître d's finger snap was like a starter pistol, and in came the white-jacketed waiters carrying the plates. They were more like platters. Covington immediately dug in. Crumbs came flying as he chewed with his mouth wide open. He loudly slurped at a glass of wine, spilling much of it. Arterial red rivulets dripped unnoticed off his chin as he reached for the plate of oysters.

He was well aware that he was breaking every rule of table etiquette. No doubts about it, he had a soft spot for food. When it came to meals, he literally became overwhelmed, almost drugged, with all the smells and tastes and, lately, even textures. He was so unabashedly gluttonous, he didn't even use silverware anymore but went at it with his bare hands like a savage in order to heighten his obsessive pleasure.

The consumption of food had become something shameless, almost horrifying, and yet in a very real sense, somehow divine. Like the famous killers Covington so admired, he possessed an intensity of desire for certain things that other people either couldn't understand or were afraid to even consider. The maître d' cleared his throat.

"More wine, sir?" he whispered beside his ear.

Covington nodded as he ripped into the duck with his bare hands, fingernails tearing deliciously at the crispy, greasy skin. "More," Covington thought, filling his mouth until his cheeks bulged. "My favorite word."

• • •

It was two in the afternoon when Covington got out of a taxi in Brooklyn's Grand Army Plaza. Dapper as can be in a chalk pinstripe Alexander McQueen power suit, he carried a brown paper bag in his right hand, and in his left his lucky cane. The razor-sharp saber inside it had a grinning pewter skull for a handle that he kept hidden under his palm as he strolled.

He arrived at 6th Avenue and made a right. A block up the leafy, brownstone-lined street, he paused by the steps of a church. He made the sign of the cross as he glanced at himself in the window of a parked Prius. He unbuttoned his jacket to show off his Hermés tie and handmade single-stitched Turnbull & Asser shirt. Now was not the time for Christian modesty. He counted the addresses until he came to 485. He stepped up the stoop and rang the doorbell with the cane.

The forty-something redheaded man who opened the door was wearing a Fordham T-shirt and shiny black basketball shorts, both speckled with primer.

"Mr. Howard?" the man said, patting at his hair as he opened the door. "What brings you here?"

"I was in the neighborhood, Kenneth," Covington said, smiling. "I remembered you lived around here and thought I'd give you a buzz."

The man's name was Kenneth Cavuto. He'd been a real estate financial analyst working for Lehman Brothers until the investment bank went belly up in the financial meltdown. Covington had interviewed the man two weeks ago after contacting him from the classifieds section of Craigslist. On the Monday following, at $200,000 to start plus bonuses, Kenneth was supposed to begin running the capital market team of Covington's fictitious new investment startup, Red Lion Investments.

"Here, I brought you a gift," Covington said, handing him the paper sack. "My mother always said when you go for a visit, ring the bell with your elbow."

"Hey, wow, thanks. You didn't have to do that," Cavuto said as he accepted the bag. "What is it?"

"Fresh strawberries and pot cheese," Covington said.

"What kind of cheese?" Cavuto said, looking into the bag.

"Pot. Though it's not the kind you're thinking of, you rascal. It's the latest thing at Whole Foods."

"Is that right? Please come in. Let me wash up, and I'll put on some coffee for me, and tea for you."

"Don't bother yourself," Covington said with a wave. "I just wanted to make sure we were buttoned down on your position. No one else has come in with a higher bid, I hope. You'll be there on Monday?"

"Of course, Mr. Howard, 9:00 a.m. sharp," the redhead assured him with a pathetic earnestness.

Covington smiled immediately as a three- or four-year-old blond girl appeared in the hall behind Cavuto.

"Hey, who's that?" Covington called to her.

"Angela? Am I right?"

"That's right. You remembered," Cavuto said with happy surprise. "Angela, come here, baby."

Covington got down on one knee as she arrived next to her father. He looked at the funny-looking doll she was holding. It was Boots the Monkey from Dora the Explorer.

"Knock, knock," Covington said to her.

"Who's there?" Angela said, peering suspiciously at him.

"Nunya."

"Nunya who?" she replied, smiling a bit.

"Nunya business," Covington said, standing. The little girl laughed. He always had a way with kids.

"Won't you come in?" Kenneth offered again.

"No, no. I'm off," Covington said. "I have to head over to the zoo in the park now, where my ex is waiting to get my little angel Bethany's fourth birthday party started and—"

Covington snapped his finger.

"Where are my manners? Why don't you come?

A couple of vice presidents from the firm will be there as well. It'll give you a chance to get acquainted before Monday."

"Really?" Cavuto said. "Sounds great. Give me five minutes to get ready."

Covington checked his flashy white gold Rolex and made a face.

"Ah, but I'm already late, and it starts off with a guided tour for the kids. The ex-wife will lay into me if I'm not right there video-recording every millisecond of it."

Covington fished into his pocket and handed Cavuto his Red Lion Investments business card.

"How's this?" Covington said. "You and Angela can skip the animals and meet us for cake."

"But, Daddy! Animals! The monkey! I want to see the monkeys," Angela said, tugging at her father's shirt and on the verge of tears.

"There I go again. Me and my big mouth," Covington said sheepishly as the girl actually started crying. He snapped his fingers.

"I feel terrible, Ken. If you want, Angela and I can start ahead so she doesn't miss the tour. Then when you're ready, call us and we'll tell you what animal we're up to."

This was the do-or-die moment, Covington knew. Hang with the boss versus parental paranoia. Covington was banking on the fact that the unemployed analyst wasn't that used to being a stay-at-home dad, was still unsure of himself, still unsure of his instincts. And, of course, if he said no, Covington would quickly switch to plan B: stun gun the father, chloroform the girl, and get out of there.

"Yeah?" Cavuto finally said.

Covington held his breath. The fish was on the hook. Time to reel it in slowly.

"You know, on second thought . . ." Covington said, checking his watch as he retreated down the stairs. The girl, sensing his departure, broke into full-fledged sobs.

"It's not too much of a pain?" Cavuto said.

"Of course not," Covington said, reaching out for

the little girl's hand with a smile. "Bethany will be so happy to make yet another brand-new best friend."

"I won't be long," Cavuto called, fingering the fake business card as they started down the sidewalk.

"Oh yes you will, Daddy," Covington thought as he waved goodbye. "Longer than you'll ever know." He turned around when they got to the corner. Cavuto had already gone back inside. Instead of heading straight for the park and the zoo, he made a left, searching for a taxi cab.

"Hey, Angela. You thirsty? Want a juice box?" Covington said, taking out the Elmo apple juice that he'd laced with liquid Valium.

"Is it 'ganic?" the white-blond-haired tot wanted to know. "Mom only likes when I drink 'ganic."

"Oh, it's 'ganic, all right, Angela," he said as a taxi pulled to the curb. "It's as 'ganic as 'ganic can be."

CHAPTER 21

THAT AFTERNOON BACK IN THE CITY, I GLUED my butt to my squad room office chair and did nothing but go through some fan mail that the prison had sent me. This guy named Berkowitz was in prison and had some information that I thought would be helpful in the case. I had asked a friend that worked there to send me some of his correspondence from people.

It was unbelievable. There were curiosity seekers, people who wanted autographs, softhearted and soft-headed religious people wanting to save the serial killer's soul. Some old cat lady from England had sent him a feline family picture along with a check for $300 to buy himself some gaspers, whatever they were. I'd have to run that by the GEICO lizard the next chance I got.

I had just gotten through all the stuff from the

2000's and was tossing my desk for some aspirin when my boss called from a Bomb Squad meeting in the Bronx.

"Something nuts just came out of Brooklyn," Miriam said. "A little girl was abducted from her dad in broad daylight. We got Brooklyn Major Case running over, but I need you to see what in the hell is going on. From the little I've heard, it's completely bizarre, which makes it par for the course for our guy. But I mean, it can't be our bastard, right? How could a child abduction have something to do with the Mad Bomber or the Grim Reaper?"

The address was in a pricey part of Brooklyn not too far from the art museum and Prospect Park. Blue-and-whites blocked both sides of the brownstone-lined street as I double-parked and headed toward an elaborately refurbished townhouse. A funereal-faced female lieutenant from the 78th Precinct met me in the bright front hallway.

"How we doing here, boss?" I said.

"We've activated the AMBER Alert and sent

Angela's picture to all the media outlets, but so far nothing," she said, lowering the static on her radio.

"How old is she?" I asked.

"The missing girl is four. Four years old, E. J. The father was totally out of it when the first unit showed, just glassy-eyed. They've got him in the back bedroom now with the mother and a doctor and a priest. A Brooklyn DT went in about five minutes ago."

Another ten long minutes passed before Hank Schaller, a veteran Brooklyn North detective who sometimes taught at the Academy, came out from the back of the house.

"Hank, what's up?" I said. The neat middle-aged man's gray eyes looked wrong as he shouldered past me like I wasn't even there. That wasn't good.

I followed him out of the townhouse and down the steps. He started speed walking down Sixth so fast I had to jog to catch up with him. He seemed in a place beyond hurt, beyond angry. Around the corner, he headed into the first place he came to, a swanky-looking restaurant. He walked around the stick-thin blond receptionist straight to the empty bar. He was loudly knocking an empty beer bottle on the black quartz bar top when I finally arrived behind him.

"I want a vodka! Yo, a fucking vodka here! Now!" he yelled.

"You some kind of asshole?" said a burly bearded guy who came in from the kitchen.

Hank was trying to launch himself over the bar at the guy when I got in front of him. I flashed my badge and dropped a twenty.

"Just get him a drink, huh?"

"This animal," Schaller whispered, crumpling onto a bar stool. He stared at the empty bottle in his hand as if wondering how it got there. "We need to catch this animal."

"What happened, Hank?"

"I can hardly even say it," he said, biting his lip. "This poor son of a bitch, the father, has been out of work for the past year, right? This guy preyed on him, said he was going to hire him. Then he shows up today out of the blue and invites both him and his daughter to his own daughter's birthday party. Cavuto's thinking, new job, new boss, definitely gotta go, right?"

The lead-assed cook finally poured three fingers of Grey Goose, which Schaller immediately knocked back.

"The dad needs a few minutes to get ready," Schaller said, raising a finger. "So the guy says he'll take the girl ahead because he's running late. Cavuto can catch up with them in ten, call to see where they are. He let her go, E. J. He gave him his kid. They walked away hand-in-hand. Except, when he gets out of his shower and calls the number, nothing happens. He runs to the zoo, and there's no party."

"What the fuck Hank?" I said. A tear ran down the bridge of the veteran's nose.

"Imagine, E. J. No one's there!"

"Take it easy, brother," I replied.

"Four years old, E. J. This girl was a butterfly.

How is this guy going to live with himself, E. J.? Fucking how?"

"You need to calm down, Hank," I tried.

"Calm down?" the cop said, flicking his tear off his cheek with his middle finger. "I know how this story ends, and so do you. I calm down when this monster is worm food. I catch up with him, this guy isn't going to see the inside of a police car, let alone a courthouse."

I watched Hank storm out of the restaurant. I stayed back in the empty bar for a second, absorbing all I'd just heard. Hank was right. Our culprit really did seem like a monster out of some primordial ooze, the personification of anti-human evil. Hank's knee-jerk reaction about it was spot on as well. What do you do when you find a nasty bug crawling up your arm? You slap it off and crush it under your foot and keep squishing it until it isn't there anymore. You do your darndest to erase it out of existence.

"That's all, Officer?" the cook said sarcastically.

"No," I said, pulling up a stool and dialing my

phone for my boss. "I need a fucking vodka now too."

I finished my drink and made some more calls before I returned to the house. Since I knew that poor Angela had been walked away, I put people on to contact the major taxi companies and the buses and subways in case anyone had seen anything.

When I arrived back at the townhouse, I spotted the CSU team and stayed out on the stoop coordinating with them. For some reason, the kidnapper had dropped off a bag with the father that contained strawberries and some kind of weird-looking cream cheese. I was hoping the bizarre package might get us a print. If this creep was bold enough to let the father get a good look at him, I was thinking, he might be getting sloppy and prone to making a mistake.

I'd just sent the department sketch artist to Detective Schaller when Emily Parker called me.

"Hey, E. J. I got the green light. Just got the word from my boss I'm on the task force."

"That couldn't be better news Emily," I said. "Because this case has just taken another left turn."

"What now?" she said.

"A four-year-old child from Brooklyn has just been abducted. I'm not sure yet how the abduction fits in with the other two sets of copycat crimes, but my gut says it's the same flavor of weird that our perp likes."

"Maybe it's another crime of the century. The Lindbergh kidnapping, maybe?" Emily said. "I'll research it and bring anything I find with me tomorrow on the train. Can you pick me up from Penn Station in the morning?"

I thought about Amy then and how I was going to manage things. It was like a fifth-grade word problem: "One love interest is waiting for you out at the beach as another one gets on a train from Washington traveling at a hundred miles an hour. How long will it take before you find yourself in the dog house?" I wasn't sure. I knew I definitely wasn't smarter than a fifth grader.

"E. J., you still there?" Emily asked.

"Right here, Emily. Of course I'll come get you. What time does it arrive?"

CHAPTER 22

NYC'S EVENING RUSH HOUR WAS JUST getting started by the time I bumper-to-bumpered it back under the arches of the Brooklyn Bridge toward my squad room. I evil-eyed my vacation-robbing workplace, One Police Plaza, as I crawled across the span. The slab concrete cube of a building had been butt ugly even before it was surrounded with guard booths and bomb-barrier planter's post 9/11.

Because traffic from the financial district had been rerouted due to all the security measures, some Chinatown businesspeople had raised a fuss and suggested that headquarters be moved to another area. I had my fingers crossed for Hawaii, but so far I hadn't heard anything.

Finally pulling off the bridge ramp onto the Avenue of the Finest, I spotted all the double-parked TV news vans. Since all the newsies and camera guys on the sidewalk beside them looked especially restless, I did myself a favor and decided to keep on going.

I drove a few blocks south and pulled over in front of a graffiti-scrawled deli on the corner of Madison and James. I got a tea and one of those slices of lemon cake and a Post, with its ever subtle tabloid headline: "WHO WILL BE NEXT?" on the front page.

Which turned out to be ironic because when I came back out onto the sidewalk, sitting on the hood of my car was Gary Aaronson, the New York Post police beat reporter who was probably responsible for the paper's headline. Like most crime reporters, Gary was ruthless. He claimed color blindness and dyslexia for his habit of ignoring crime scene tape.

So instead of heading back for my vehicle, I hooked a hard left and stepped into Jerry's Old School, an inner-city barbershop I sometimes used as a meeting spot with confidential informants. I almost tripped over Cathy Calvin, the New York Times police beat reporter by the door, under a poster for the rapper Uncle Murder.

I glared over at the muscular owner, Jerry, giving some Chinese kid a fade.

"Is nothing sacred, my man?" I asked him as I did an immediate 180 back outside.

Calvin had exchanged her phone for a tape recorder by the time she caught up to me on the sidewalk.

"We have a bombing spree, a double murder that looks a lot like the Grim Reaper, and now a girl is missing. Rumors are that all three are related. What's going on, Detective?"

As if I had the time to perform in the media circus.

"Didn't I blackball you?" I said as I picked up my pace.

"That was just for the last case," Calvin said.

"Finally," Aaronson said, taking out his own recorder as he got off the hood of my Marquis.

"I got this one, Gary," Calvin said, waving him

away.

The Post reporter stepped away, making "call me" gestures at Calvin. All the newspaper hacks who covered crime hung out together. They were as thick as thieves and just about as considerate when it came to cops. They actually had some space on the 2nd floor of HQ called the Shack, where they came up with new ways to get cases and cops jammed up.

"No, she doesn't, Gary," I said, opening my car door. "You want info? Talk to the 13th floor, Cathy, my lass. I'm sure they'll be willing to hand over everything you need to know."

The 13th floor was home to the department's Public Information Office. Because of the logjam in the white-hot case, its under-pressure chief wanted certain vital body parts of mine for breakfast, last I'd heard.

"C'mon, E. J. I do news, not propaganda," Calvin said, rolling her eyes.

"That's not what Fox News says," I shot back before I jumped into the safety of my vehicle.

I was starting the car to make my escape when the passenger door opened and Calvin hopped in beside me.

"What class of medication did you forget to take this morning?" I asked.

"I'm screwed, E. J." she replied, letting out a weary breath. "I'm not kidding. You don't understand how desperate things are in the paper biz right now, especially now that there's social media. The city editor is waiting for any tiny excuse to clear up some payroll. Can't you give me anything? I'll take a 'no comment' at this point."

"In that case, no comment," I said as I leaned across her and opened her door. "Good sob story, by the way. I almost fell for it. The first three times you used it. You should update it. Toss in a dying roommate or something."

"You really are heartless, aren't you?" Calvin said.

"Heartless, yes. A sucker, no," I said. "If it bleeds, it leads, right, Cathy? This one is most definitely bleeding. The last thing I'm worried about is your job security." She gave me a thin smile.

"Fine, fine. I like you, too, by the way, E. J. Hard as it is to believe. What's that cologne you're wearing? I like it."

I sniffed. It was some Axe body soap one of my kids had left in the sand-covered shower back at Breezy. It actually did smell pretty good. I knew she was just yanking my chain to get an angle on the case. Or was she?

"Cathy Calvin, you seem like a nice enough young woman," I said. "You're educated. You dress nice. I thought covering cops was just a stepping stone to better things. Is it the street cred? You have a thing for dead bodies? You ever ask yourself?"

"Come to dinner with me and find out, E. J.," she said, checking her makeup in my rearview. "I'll tell you the long, sad story over a bottle of wine. I'm partial to Jameson myself."

Then she gave me a naughty girl stare for a few seconds. Cathy Calvin was a tall, slim blonde with soft green eyes. I couldn't help staring back.

"We won't even talk shop. I promise," she said, clicking off her tape recorder with a red-nailed thumb. She smiled. "Well, maybe just a teensy, weensy bit."

It was the click that did it. It snapped me back to what was left of my senses. What the hell was I doing or thinking? Attractive or not, Cathy was nuts and the enemy. Even if she wasn't, I had a beautiful woman at home and another that was coming in from Washington.

"Some other time, Calvin," I said. "If you haven't noticed, I'm a tad busy these days."

"Whatever you say, Detective," she said, getting out. She stopped for a moment on the sidewalk and turned slowly, giving me a good look at what I'd be missing. "My phone is always on."

"I'm sure it is," I mumbled as I pretended to ignore her walking away.

CHAPTER 23

AFTER ANOTHER THREE FRUITLESS HOURS spent fishing through the Grim Reaper letters at my desk, I was toast. I was about to leave when I received a call from Miriam telling me that the commissioner was on his way back from a speech in Philadelphia and wanted me to brief him in person. So I stuck around for another two hours at my desk, only to have Miriam call back to say that the big Kahuna had actually changed his mind and I was free to go.

I thought my day was over, but Seamus called me on my cell phone and told me to meet him at the Flaherty house. I was wondering why, but he told me that he had arranged a sit-down. It was weird that he would do that, but I met him over there. How the hell did I get myself into these things?

When I pulled up, Seamus was standing outside.

He had on his black jeans and a black T-shirt. We knocked on the door. When no one answered, we decided to go around the side of the house to the back. The sulfurous smell of gunpowder hung in the air, which I thought was fitting, since we were now walking through the valley of the shadow of death, straight into the gates of hell.

The rear of the place was almost completely overtaken by a very large deck and one of those cheap above-ground pools. Tommy Boy, as he was known, sat with his tattooed brother Billy. I realized why no one had called the cops when I saw the third Flaherty for the first time. I didn't know what his name was, but I noticed that he was still wearing his white NYPD captain's shirt as he tossed a lit bottle rocket toward the house next door. Tommy looked at us.

"What the—?" he said. His pale face split into a grin. "Hey, guys. Check this out. How's this for a joke: a cop and a priest walk uninvited into a private party."

"We're here to have that sit-down, Flaherty," Seamus said. "We're not leaving until we have that talk."

"Sit-down?" the illustrated Flaherty brother, Billy, said, balling his hands into a fist as he stood. "Only thing that's gonna happen to you, coot, is a serious beatdown."

"Murphy sent me," Seamus said to Tommy Boy, completely ignoring the tattooed man.

"Murphy?" Tommy Boy said, not budging from his cheap plastic chair. "Frank Murphy? That dirty ol' little Forty-Ninth Street bookie I let operate out of the kindness of my heart? News flash, Father Moron. He's less valid than you and your son. Now get your scrawny ass out of here before my brother Billy here makes it so that you have to say mass for the rest of your life in a wheelchair."

As the tattooed brother took a step toward us, I decided it was time to take the lead. My first move was to gently push Seamus to the side. My next and last move was to much less gently kick the seated

Flaherty in the side of the head as hard as I could as I drew my Glock.

I helped him up by his long, greasy hair, the barrel of my gun wedged into his ear hole like a pencil into a sharpener.

"Morris! Whoa, whoa, hold up," the cop brother said, slowly showing me his hands. "We don't need this kind of stuff. We're all friends here. You worked with my old partner, Joe Kelly, when you were still in Philly. You came out here to help over in Manhattan North Homicide."

"That's right, I worked homicide," I said. "And I'm not above committing one right about now. Three of them, in fact. How's this for a joke, Flaherty? Three dumb-ass brothers are found floating facedown dead in their own fucking pool."

"Let me get this straight. You're actually willing to shoot me over this stupid kiddie crap?" Tommy Boy asked from the other side of my Glock. I nodded enthusiastically.

"Your kid almost killed my seven-year-old

tonight at the carnival. To protect my kids, you better believe I'll end your worthless ass."

"I see," Tommy Boy said, looking at me sideways across the gun I was scratching against his eardrum. "I hadn't heard about that. I think I'm starting to understand your position now. I even know what to do. Here, watch. Seany!"

The screen door opened a few moments later, and the fat kid who'd been terrorizing my family stepped out onto the deck. His pudgy jaw dropped in a cartoonish gape when he saw me and his dad down on the deck conversing over the barrel of my Austrian semi-auto.

"Uh . . . yes, Dad?" he said, fear in his voice.

"Come here," Flaherty senior said.

Quick as a snake, Tommy Boy moved out of my grasp before the kid had made two steps. Before I could tell what was going on, he lifted his portly son up and threw him off the deck. Instead of landing in the pool, like I was expecting, the heavy teen slammed into the side of it with a cracking sound before he fell face-first onto the backyard concrete. Right away he started bawling. "Christ," I thought, standing there shocked, with the gun still in my hand, "Now, that's what you call tough love."

"Dad!" young Sean cried from his knees as blood poured out of his nose. Behind him, water began to trickle out of the crack he'd made in the plastic pool.

"Don't you Dad me, you little punk. Stay the hell away from this man's kids, you hear me?"

"But, Dad," Seany wheezed. "You told me to teach them a lesson."

"Yeah, well," Tommy Boy said, giving me a sheepish look. "Lesson learned. You don't hurt little kids, shithead. I have to actually explain that to you? Here's the new orders. If one of Mr. Morris's kids skins his or her knee, you better have a Band-Aid handy. Any of them gets hurt again, and you're going to spend the rest of your vacation in the hospital."

"Yes, Dad," Seany moaned as he ran up the deck stairs and back inside.

"Honestly, Morris," Flaherty said with his palms

up. "I'm sorry about the whole thing. It really is my fault. My wife went to Ireland for a week to bury her mother. Guess I'm not so great at this dad thing. Everything's just gone to hell without her here."

"There's a definite learning curve," I said, reholstering my weapon. "I'm just glad we could finally work things out."

"Man to man," Seamus added behind me.

"Hey, it took a lot of guts to come over here. I respect that," Tommy Boy said as we were leaving. "You ever need anything, anything, you let me know. That goes for you, too, Father."

"Back, Satan," Seamus mumbled as we took our leave.

I let out the breath of all breaths as I got the car started. Pulling my gun had been beyond reckless. What the hell had gotten into me? As we drove away, I suddenly got a proud pat on the cheek from Seamus.

"We'll make a man out of you yet, E. J., me boy." He winked and smiled. "That's how you do things around here."

CHAPTER 24

NAKED IN THE DARK, COVINGTON KICKED back on the leather recliner in his massive, magnificent library and hit the Play button on his remote control. There was a chirp and hum from the Blu-ray player and then the 103-inch plasma blazed with a midday shot of the New York Public Library.

The camera shook a little from the first person shot, but the picture, colors, and sounds of the street were amazingly vivid. You could almost smell the hot pretzels and summer sweat. It was the film of the first crime, the library decoy bombing that had been shot with a hidden fiber-optic camera. All of his work, of course, had been filmed.

Now it was time to edit it, clean it up, and polish, polish, polish. As the images fast-forwarded and rewound, he thought of his school years at Lawrenceville, the premier boarding school near

Princeton. A pudgy and slow child, he had been enrolled by his father at the über-preppy institution in order to make a gentleman out of him, but it didn't work out. Quite the contrary.

By the time Covington entered ninth grade, his physique, unique artistic sensibilities, and uncommon interests had actually earned him an alliterative nickname that had caught on famously: Big Bellied Bizarro Covington.

He was seriously considering suicide for his fifteenth birthday, when he unexpectedly made a friend. His new roommate, Javier Sousa, a diminutive boy from a wealthy Brazilian family, not only called him by his name, but he turned out to share some of his strange, dark interests.

It was Javier who dared him to burn down the school library during the freshman class movie night the week before Christmas break. Wanting to prove his mettle, Covington had purchased a case of lighter fluid as well as some lengths of chain and padlocks to bar the building's exits.

If the suspicious owner of the Ace Hardware store in town hadn't contacted the headmaster, he would have gone through with his plan of wiping out the entire Lawrenceville class of '68. Instead, he was expelled, and if it hadn't been for a hasty and hefty donation by his father to the school, there might have been criminal charges.

"Coulda, woulda, shoulda," Covington thought wistfully. He'd had such passion then. If it hadn't been for the hand of fate, he would have become famous then. He would have instantly transformed from Big Bellied Bizarro Covington to the Boy Who Killed the Class of '68!

It was, of course, that singular near brush with greatness that drove him on his little project now. After all the failure and misery and confusion that had clouded his life, he'd finally, miraculously, gotten his gumption back.

In the light of the TV screen, he dabbed at a joyful tear as he watched the bomb get glued to the library desk. What he had done already, the sheer wondrousness of it, no one could ever take away. No matter what happened next, he had triumphed. Covington had finally done something that was truly his.

•   •   •

Though it was only 9:00 a.m., I felt punch drunk by the time I pulled up in front of Madison Square Garden on Seventh Avenue to pick up Agent Parker at Penn Station. Horns honked as I blatantly and highly illegally sat in my cruiser in a no-standing tow zone, washing down a bagel with a Big Gulp-size coffee.

As the loud, cruel world rushed by the window, I slowly went over what had happened with the Flahertys the night before. Talk about fireworks! I'd broken a few laws there, hadn't I? Improper use of a firearm was a firing offense. Assault was a felony, but I guess the strangest thing about it was that it seemed to have worked. At the time I really didn't care about the consequences anyway. It was about protecting my family.

I'd finally spoken to Flaherty in the only language he seemed to understand. Why hadn't I just threatened his life from the get-go? I shook my head. I'd actually out-crazied a Westie. Was that a good thing? I wasn't sure, but probably not.

The grind of the case wasn't exactly doing wonders for my mental well-being, was it? I needed a vacation. Oh, wait, I was already on one. I flipped through the Post. On page 3, a state senator from Manhattan warned that the NYPD had five more days to catch the culprit before he made a motion that the state police be sent in. Sounded good to me, I thought, licking my thumb and turning the page.

I would be more than happy to let a trooper from Schenectady take a shot at cracking the case. In addition to the mayor, the papers, and the department top brass, I was almost starting to want me off this case too. I knew the odds were we'd eventually catch up to this monster. I'd caught up to every one of them so far. I knew I should believe the numbers on the back of my baseball card, and yet I was getting very worried. Especially about Angela Cavuto.

There had been no word yet from her kidnapper, no demands. No news was definitely not good news. The one bright spot was the new sketch of the kidnapper the department artist had made with the help of Mr. Cavuto. They'd red balled it to the Public Info Division this morning to get it out on the newscasts, so maybe we had a shot. How much of one, I wasn't sure. But at least it was a start.

After another few minutes, I checked the time on my phone and got out of the car, leaving it right in the middle of the Seventh Avenue bus lane. If I got towed, maybe they'd let me get back to my vacation, I thought as I took the escalator from the sidewalk down into Penn Station. I really didn't think anything could cut through my darkening mood until I saw Emily Parker's smile and wave on the crowded underground train platform. She looked even better than I remembered.

She was tall and porcelain-skinned, her eyes as

bright and blue as ever. Her neatness and earnestness and energy were contagious. I think I actually smiled back as we came face-to-face. We hugged, and she even gave me a peck on the cheek. Not exactly FBI protocol. It felt good.

"Finally some backup," I said, grabbing her bag. "Honestly, Emily, you are a sight for these sore eyes."

"It's nice to see you too, E. J.," she said, giving my hand another squeeze. "It really is. I'm glad I came. You look great."

"Yeah, real GQ, I'm sure," I said, rolling my eyes. "The bags under my eyes are bigger than your overnight."

"But such handsome luggage," she replied, giving my cheek a playful tug.

I grinned back at her like a fool. Demonstrative attention from good-looking women was never a bad thing for me. Our reunion was off on the right foot. So far, so good.

"What do you want to do first?"

"Brainstorm," I said, leading her toward the stairs. "But we're going to need to use your brain. I fried mine about three days ago."

CHAPTER
25

TWENTY MINUTES LATER, EMILY AND I WERE standing in the center of Major Case Squad's open bullpen on the 11th floor of One Police Plaza. Phones kept ringing across the stuffy, beat-up empty office space, with nobody to answer them. Every single one of the task force's forty-plus detectives was out chasing down leads on the now three-pronged case. There was no rest for the weary in this summer of insanity. Nor any in sight, for that matter.

Beyond the cluster of cluttered desks, we parked ourselves in front of a decidedly low-tech rolling bulletin board. Pushpinned onto it was a huge map of the city, along with the printouts of each crime and crime scene. In the very center of the board, the new Xeroxed sketch of the kidnapper stared back at us like a spider from the center of its web.

With her arms crossed, Emily stared at the board

silently, absorbed, an art critic before a new install-
lation.

"Give me the vitals on the abduction, E. J."

I slowly went through what had happened to
Angela Cavuto.

"According to the father," I said, "our guy is
white, right-handed, walks with a limp and a cane,
and is thin and about five eleven. Cavuto also said he
was cultured and polished. Not only was he wearing
a tailored suit, but he spoke quite convincingly about
hedge fund investing."

"I can't believe it, E. J.," Emily told me as she
took a rubber-banded folder out of her bag. "I spent
yesterday pulling reams of stuff about famous New
York crimes, hoping this wasn't true, but I think it
must be."

"What have you got, Emily?"

"I think this guy's done it again. This abduction
is another copycat. A carbon copy, in fact."

"Of what? The Lindbergh case?" I asked,
confused.

"No. There was another heinous kidnapping way back in the '20s, in Brooklyn. At the time, they called it the crime of the century."

"I think I remember that," I stated.

"Yeah, a sociopathic murderous pedophile named Albert Fish was dubbed the Brooklyn Vampire when he abducted and killed a girl."

"And E. J., his MO wasn't just similar. From what you just told me, it was exactly the same. Posing as an employer, Fish answered the ad of an eighteen-year-old boy seeking work and ended up leaving with his ten-year-old sister under the pretense of taking her to a birthday party."

"F—off! No!" I yelled as I collapsed into a chair. Emily nodded.

"Tell me, did he give the father something?" she said.

"Strawberries and some goop," I replied.

"Pot cheese. Right. Shit! It's the same thing! The Mad Bomber, then the Grim Reaper, now the Brooklyn Vampire. This guy's just pulled off a third famous crime. E. J., this isn't good. This Fish guy was evil personified. He made the Grim Reaper seem like a volunteer at a soup kitchen. He was one of the worst pedophiles and child murderers of all time. He didn't just kill his victims, he would cannibalize them as well."

I punched the desk beside me, then my thigh. Then Emily and I sat there silently listening to the whoosh of the air duct. On the board, a picture of Angela from last year's Cavuto family Christmas card smiled at us from beneath a glittery halo.

• • •

I was with Emily, putting on some coffee about an hour later, when I heard a strange, gut-wrenching call come over the break room's radio. There was some kind of disturbance uptown. An unconscious, unresponsive child had been found in a store on Fifth Avenue. When I heard the name of the store repeated, my blood went cold.

"What, E. J.? What is it?" Emily said, straining

to listen.

"They found a little girl uptown at FAO Schwartz, the famous toy store across from the Plaza Hotel. Not good, Em. It's on the same block as the CBS Early Show."

"What?"

"That was the locale of the bombing on Tuesday."

There was a more massive crowd than usual out in front of the landmark toy store when we arrived after a long, twenty-minute ride uptown. Two radio cars and two ambulances spun their lights in front of the freaked-out-looking tourists and moms and little kids. A veteran 19th Precinct sergeant whose eye I caught shook his dismal face before I was three steps out of my car. I showed the cop the picture of Angela.

"Tell me this isn't her," I said.

"Marone a mi," the cop said, the smoke from his cigarette rising like incense as he crossed himself. "It's her. They found her in the back. The clerk thought she was just sleeping."

Emily and I both turned as a car squealed up behind my parked cruiser. It was a black Lexus with tinted windows. I had my hand on my Glock when its door was flung wide open and a man got out. A man with red hair and even redder eyes. It was Kenneth Cavuto, Angela's father.

"No!" I yelled as Cavuto bolted toward the store's entrance.

I managed to get there a second before him. No way could I let Angela's dad see his little girl. Not here, and like that. Apparently the distraught father had other plans. I'm not a small guy when it comes to muscles, but Cavuto shoved me off my feet like I was an empty cardboard box. I grunted as I fell forward and my chin hit the concrete.

I got back up and ran after Cavuto into the empty store. I bolted down some steps past museum-quality displays of giant stuffed animals: ostriches and horses and giraffes. I was scrambling past the Puppet Park when I heard a sound that stopped me. It was a scream in a pitch I'd never heard before. I looked at

Emily. She shook her head. We both knew what it was. It was the sound of Cavuto's heart breaking. It took me, Emily, and three uniforms to get Cavuto off his daughter. I actually had to cuff him.

He started crying soundlessly as he banged his head against the polka-dot-carpeted floor. I felt so bad for him, and there was nothing I could do.

"Go out to your truck and get something to knock this poor son of a bitch out, would you?" I yelled at a gawking EMT.

I noticed only then that my chin was bleeding. I put my thumb on it to stop the drip as I turned and looked at the girl. She was sitting in a stroller with her eyes closed, her white-blond hair the same shade as the oversize polar bear on the shelf beside her. I turned away and got down on my knees next to the father and placed my hand on his sobbing back. I opened my mouth to say something. Then I closed it. What was there to say? I knew I needed to catch this creep though. He was causing too much pain and grief, to too many families.

CHAPTER
26

THE EVENING LIGHT WAS JUST STARTING TO change as Covington steered the Mercedes convertible into the line for the car wash at East 109th Street. He stared up at the fading blue of the sky above the construction site across the street. What he wouldn't give to be in his tub right now, humming on Vitamin P as the sun descended toward the Dakota.

He turned as an unshaven bubble-butted old white guy knocked on his window. Covington thought it was a homeless person until he realized it was one of the car wash employees.

"What?" the guy asked in a Russian accent as the window buzzed down.

"The works," Covington said, handing him a crisp twenty.

"Interior vacuum too?" Gorbachev wanted to

know.

"Not today," Covington replied with a grin before zipping the window back up.

Covington sighed as the machinery bumped under the car and began towing him through the spinning brushes and water spray. What a bust of a day. The girl wasn't supposed to die. The plan had been to torture the parents over a two-day period with the ruse of a ransom and then kill her. But that was all blown to shit now, wasn't it?

It had been the Valium. The girl had had some kind of allergic reaction as he was taking her from the taxi to the Mercedes that he had parked in Brooklyn Heights. By the time they were back in Manhattan, she was gone. He'd screwed up, made his first mistake. He could kick himself.

"Oh well," he thought as the lemony scent of soap filled the car. He had to stop beating himself up about it because no mission went perfectly. He smoothed out the fiber optic camera cord sewn into the lining of his jacket. At the very least he'd gotten a little more footage. Anyway, he didn't have time to dwell on his failures. So much to do, so little time to do it. He'd just have to go on to the next thing.

He needed to keep heading in his two favorite directions, onward and upward, and hope it would all come out in the wash. As the car wash spat him back out into the driveway, he rolled down the window and tossed something into the trash can by the fence. The Elmo juice box spun as it arced lazily into the can's exact center. Boots the Monkey followed.

"Swish! Nothing but net, and the crowd goes wild," Covington said as he stepped on the accelerator and squealed the Mercedes out into the street.

•   •   •

After his preliminary, the ME took me aside by a stack of Buzz Lightyears and said it looked like an overdose of some kind. I turned away as a crying female ME assistant knelt by Angela, getting ready to move her. Her father, mercifully sedated, was out in an ambulance on East 58th. I wished I were as well.

"What do you think?" I said to Emily as we stepped along the rows of toys for the exit. "Does this dump fit in with the Fish case in some way?"

"No, actually," Emily said. "They found his victim's remains in an abandoned house upstate. My gut says our unsub screwed up, probably botched the dosage trying to keep her quiet."

"Sounds about right," I said as we arrived back out in the street. I was hoping the outside air would make me feel better, but the crowds and heat only made me feel shittier.

"Guess our copycatting friend isn't Mr. Perfect after all," I said.

We left the amazingly sad and angering crime scene about an hour later. I took Fifth Avenue south from FAO Schwartz and hooked a right at Thirty-Fourth, by the Empire State Building.

"It's weird," Emily said, squeezing the empty water bottle in her hand as she stared at the sketch.

"He's definitely culturally sophisticated, and yet he also has military training, judging by his bomb-making skills. Interesting combination."

"Don't forget, he's also quite the New York City crime buff," I said.

"Speaking of which," Emily said, turning and taking out a folder from her bag. "You guys probably thought of this, but before I hopped on the train, I printed out a custom map for all the crime scenes of the Mad Bomber and the Grim Reaper that I could scratch together off the web. There are dozens in Manhattan, the Bronx, everywhere except Staten Island. It's a long shot, but beefed-up patrols at some of these potential target neighborhoods might get us some luck."

I smiled at the neat Google pinpointed map and then at Agent Parker. Emily was exactly what this case needed: a new set of eyes, some new blood, some enthusiasm. Back at the office, a stocky, young black detective dressed like Gordon Gekko all the way down to a pair of silk suspenders almost tackled us as we got off the elevator. His name was Terry Brown, and he was the squad's latest rookie out of Narcotics.

"E. J., finally," Terry said, waving for us to follow him. "I just got through the toy store security tape. I think I might have something. You have to see this."

Me and Emily followed Terry down the hall and into one of the tiny interview rooms, where he was banished until Maintenance found him a desk. Through a corridor of stacked file boxes, we huddled together at a folding table as he pressed the play button on his laptop. He fast-forwarded through people browsing among the toy-filled shelves and then hit Pause as a man with a stroller entered the frame.

"There he is. Now watch."

The man came closer, pushing the same pink Maclaren stroller Angela was found in. I let out a whooshing breath. He was wearing a Yankees cap and a pair of aviator shades, but it was him, the guy from the sketch! For the first time, I was face-to-face with the man responsible for killing eight people over the past few days and terrorizing another eight million.

He wheeled her into a corner. He took out his cellphone from his pocket and took a picture of her. What really burned my ass was how he actually stopped and then glanced up at the security camera and smiled as he left the store.

"That son of a bitch," I said. "He knew the camera was there. He's taunting us now."

We played it over and over again, trying to get the best shot. It turned out to be the one of him smiling.

"I did good?" Terry Brown asked hopefully.

"You keep this up, Terry," I said to the pup, pumped for the first time all day. "Not only will I get you a desk, but I might also even throw in a chair."

After firing our latest findings to the AV guys on the 3rd floor, they blew up the image and did a terrific side-by-side with the sketch. Even better, the

Public Info Office said they'd hustle and get it into today's evening news cycle.

When we left headquarters, I was about to take Emily over to her hotel so she could check in, when I received a call.

"Morris," I answered.

"Turn on the news now," one of the detectives from my squad said.

"Come on," I said, pulling Emily back inside.

I spotted a television and turned it on. Soon as I got the news station, both me and Emily's mouth dropped open. There was another bombing. This time, it was a police station. People were scrambling all over the place trying to get out of there. Police officer's bodies were lying on the ground, some burnt to a crisp. It was hard to watch.

"Oh my God, E. J. This is terrible," Emily said with her hand over her mouth.

"We have to get this son of a bitch," I said, tears forming in my eyes from the sight of seeing my fellow officers dying right before my eyes. "He's a dead man . . ."

TO BE CONTINUED!!

The Author

Ernest E. J. Morris has created more enduring fictional characters than he can count. He is the author of the Flipping Numbers series, and the Naughty Housewives series, two of his most popular series today. Some of his other novels include:

Trapped in Love, Supreme and Justice, Deadly Reunion, A Hustler's Dream, Killing Signs, Money Makes Me Cum, Black Reign, Lost and Turned Out, Forbidden Passion, The Betrayal Within, and *Death by Association.*

Ernest Morris has also written a book called *Breaking the Chains*, which focuses on teaching young kids how to stay out of trouble. He shares his own life experiences, with the hopes of saving the next generation. His lifelong passion for writing has helped him through good and bad times. He writes full-time and lives in Pennsylvania.

If you would like to contact him, you can follow him on Facebook at: EJMORRIS or Instagram at: EJFLIPPIN, or you can email him at: EJMORRIS2020@gmail.com.

To order books, please fill out the order form below:
To order films please go to www.good2gofilms.com

Name:_____

Address:_____

City:_____State:_____Zip Code: _____

Phone:_____

Email:_____

Method of Payment: Check   VISA MASTERCARD

Credit Card#:_ _____

Name as it appears on card: _____

Signature: _____

Item Name	Price	Qty	Amount
48 Hours to Die – Silk White	$14.99		
A Hustler's Dream – Ernest Morris	$14.99		
A Hustler's Dream 2 – Ernest Morris	$14.99		
A Thug's Devotion – J. L. Rose and J. M. McMillon	$14.99		
All Eyes on Tommy Gunz – Warren Holloway	$14.99		
Black Reign – Ernest Morris	$14.99		
Bloody Mayhem Down South – Trayvon Jackson	$14.99		
Bloody Mayhem Down South 2 – Trayvon Jackson	$14.99		
Business Is Business – Silk White	$14.99		
Business Is Business 2 – Silk White	$14.99		
Business Is Business 3 – Silk White	$14.99		
Cash In Cash Out – Assa Raymond Baker	$14.99		
Cash In Cash Out 2 – Assa Raymond Baker	$14.99		
Childhood Sweethearts – Jacob Spears	$14.99		
Childhood Sweethearts 2 – Jacob Spears	$14.99		
Childhood Sweethearts 3 – Jacob Spears	$14.99		
Childhood Sweethearts 4 – Jacob Spears	$14.99		
Connected To The Plug – Dwan Marquis Williams	$14.99		
Connected To The Plug 2 – Dwan Marquis Williams	$14.99		
Connected To The Plug 3 – Dwan Williams	$14.99		
Cost of Betrayal – W.C. Holloway	$14.99		
Cost of Betrayal 2 – W.C. Holloway	$14.99		
Deadly Reunion – Ernest Morris	$14.99		
Dream's Life – Assa Raymond Baker	$14.99		
Flipping Numbers – Ernest Morris	$14.99		
Flipping Numbers 2 – Ernest Morris	$14.99		

Forbidden Pleasure – Ernest Morris	$14.99		
He Loves Me, He Loves You Not – Mychea	$14.99		
He Loves Me, He Loves You Not 2 – Mychea	$14.99		
He Loves Me, He Loves You Not 3 – Mychea	$14.99		
He Loves Me, He Loves You Not 4 – Mychea	$14.99		
He Loves Me, He Loves You Not 5 – Mychea	$14.99		
Killing Signs – Ernest Morris	$14.99		
Killing Signs 2 – Ernest Morris	$14.99		
Kings of the Block – Dwan Willams	$14.99		
Kings of the Block 2 – Dwan Willams	$14.99		
Lord of My Land – Jay Morrison	$14.99		
Lost and Turned Out – Ernest Morris	$14.99		
Love & Dedication – W.C. Holloway	$14.99		
Love Hates Violence – De'Wayne Maris	$14.99		
Love Hates Violence 2 – De'Wayne Maris	$14.99		
Love Hates Violence 3 – De'Wayne Maris	$14.99		
Love Hates Violence 4 – De'Wayne Maris	$14.99		
Married To Da Streets – Silk White	$14.99		
M.E.R.C. – Make Every Rep Count Health and Fitness	$14.99		
Mercenary In Love – J.L. Rose & J.L. Turner	$14.99		
Money Make Me Cum – Ernest Morris	$14.99		
My Besties – Asia Hill	$14.99		
My Besties 2 – Asia Hill	$14.99		
My Besties 3 – Asia Hill	$14.99		
My Besties 4 – Asia Hill	$14.99		
My Boyfriend's Wife – Mychea	$14.99		
My Boyfriend's Wife 2 – Mychea	$14.99		
My Brothers Envy – J. L. Rose	$14.99		
My Brothers Envy 2 – J. L. Rose	$14.99		
Naughty Housewives – Ernest Morris	$14.99		
Naughty Housewives 2 – Ernest Morris	$14.99		
Naughty Housewives 3 – Ernest Morris	$14.99		
Naughty Housewives 4 – Ernest Morris	$14.99		
Never Be The Same – Silk White	$14.99		
Scarred Faces – Assa Raymond Baker	$14.99		

Scarred Knuckles – Assa Raymond Baker	$14.99		
Secrets in the Dark – Ernest Morris	$14.99		
Shades of Revenge – Assa Raymond Baker	$14.99		
Slumped – Jason Brent	$14.99		
Someone's Gonna Get It – Mychea	$14.99		
Stranded – Silk White	$14.99		
Supreme & Justice – Ernest Morris	$14.99		
Supreme & Justice 2 – Ernest Morris	$14.99		
Supreme & Justice 3 – Ernest Morris	$14.99		
Tears of a Hustler – Silk White	$14.99		
Tears of a Hustler 2 – Silk White	$14.99		
Tears of a Hustler 3 – Silk White	$14.99		
Tears of a Hustler 4 – Silk White	$14.99		
Tears of a Hustler 5 – Silk White	$14.99		
Tears of a Hustler 6 – Silk White	$14.99		
The Betrayal Within – Ernest Morris	$14.99		
The Last Love Letter – Warren Holloway	$14.99		
The Last Love Letter 2 – Warren Holloway	$14.99		
The Panty Ripper – Reality Way	$14.99		
The Panty Ripper 3 – Reality Way	$14.99		
The Solution – Jay Morrison	$14.99		
The Teflon Queen – Silk White	$14.99		
The Teflon Queen 2 – Silk White	$14.99		
The Teflon Queen 3 – Silk White	$14.99		
The Teflon Queen 4 – Silk White	$14.99		
The Teflon Queen 5 – Silk White	$14.99		
The Teflon Queen 6 – Silk White	$14.99		
The Vacation – Silk White	$14.99		
The Webpage Murder – Ernest Morris	$14.99		
The Webpage Murder 2 – Ernest Morris	$14.99		
Tied To A Boss – J.L. Rose	$14.99		
Tied To A Boss 2 – J.L. Rose	$14.99		
Tied To A Boss 3 – J.L. Rose	$14.99		
Tied To A Boss 4 – J.L. Rose	$14.99		
Tied To A Boss 5 – J.L. Rose	$14.99		
Time Is Money – Silk White	$14.99		

Tomorrow's Not Promised – Robert Torres	$14.99		
Tomorrow's Not Promised 2 – Robert Torres	$14.99		
Two Mask One Heart – Jacob Spears and Trayvon Jackson	$14.99		
Two Mask One Heart 2 – Jacob Spears and Trayvon Jackson	$14.99		
Two Mask One Heart 3 – Jacob Spears and Trayvon Jackson	$14.99		
Wife – Assa Ray Baker & Raneissa Baker	$14.99		
Wife 2 – Assa Ray Baker & Raneissa Baker	$14.99		
Wrong Place Wrong Time – Silk White	$14.99		
Young Goonz – Reality Way	$14.99		
Subtotal:			
Tax:			
Shipping (Free) U.S. Media Mail:			
Total:			

Make Checks Payable To Good2Go Publishing, 7311 W Glass Lane, Laveen, AZ 85339

CPSIA information can be obtained
at www.ICGtesting.com
Printed in the USA
LVHW010937230821
695886LV00002B/193